Find This Woman

Find This
Woman

Richard S. Prather

OPEN ROAD
INTEGRATED MEDIA
NEW YORK

ISBN 978-1-4976-3732-0

This edition published in 2014 by Open Road Integrated Media, Inc.
345 Hudson Street
New York, NY 10014
www.openroadmedia.com

For Tina

Find This Woman

1

S HE STILL had all her clothes on and was standing in the blue light from a baby spot when I came in, but I knew it wasn't going to last because the way she was moving I could tell it was that kind of dance. I was glad it was that kind of dance.

It was a few minutes before one o'clock in the morning and I'd just run in under the tan awning of the Pelican Club in downtown Gardena, twelve miles south of Los Angeles, found the headwaiter I'd called earlier, and told him I was Shell Scott. I gave him his damned ten dollars and followed him toward the little ringside table I'd just paid for. Nobody looked at me.

The MC or owner or some other idiot must have had a microphone offstage somewhere, because he was still talking and saying that all fire regulations had been complied with and that men were standing by with extinguishers so that there was nothing, absolutely nothing, to be afraid of. If I hadn't come here specifically to talk to the lovely getting ready to dance a few feet from me, I might have turned around, asked for my ten back, and left. I was thinking that if the gags were that old and tired, the dance would probably be a minuet, but then I heard the idiot say something about a fire dance and scream happily, ". . . and here she is!"

Hell, she'd been there for half a minute. But now I understood that what I'd thought was a corny gag wasn't a gag at all, and that the anonymous voice

1

had merely been trying in a feeble way to build suspense with the old show-business hyperbole. There was some fire, but it was nothing to call the department about.

Even though the waiter brought my bourbon and water in a hurry—probably because he wanted to watch, too—I barely had time to ease my six foot two inches into my chair, look the place over, and take one swallow of my drink before the shapely lady out there really went into her routine and I lost interest in everything else. I thought I needed a drink then; I was going to need it more before she finished dancing.

This was the feature act of the last show and the elaborate props had already been set up. My table was right at one of the corners of the dance floor and I could look straight back to the stand where the orchestra was playing. I couldn't see the orchestra, though, because one of the props was a big cloth or paper screen about fifteen feet square that had already been placed in front of the musicians. The screen was crudely painted in bright reds and greens and yellows with the figure of a great and obscene Buddha-like idol sitting cross-legged with his fleshy hands folded over his distended abdomen. Just this side of the painted background, rising two or three feet up from the floor, was some kind of wall, indistinct in the blue spotlight, and from behind it and extending almost all the way across the floor from my left to my right, twenty or thirty tiny fingers of fire wavered unsteadily. Probably natural gas or some inflammable liquid was piped in, but the thing was putting out about as much flame as a handful of matches. Even so, the whole thing, with the girl swaying in the blue light of the spot before the gross idol towering above her, and the little flames glowing between her and the idol, was pretty effective.

She was gliding across the polished dance floor toward my table now, so I took a good look at her. All I knew about her was that she was billed as "Sweet Lorraine" and that she did some kind of dancing and that this was the delightful young woman I'd come here to talk to, and that at no time in the history of "Sheldon Scott, Investigations," had a case started in a more interesting fashion. Because Lorraine certainly was making it interesting.

She was wide-hipped and full-breasted like a Ben Stahl illustration for a wanton dancing in hell, and if she'd done this dance in hell, the devil himself would have flipped. She was about five-six or five-seven, and so close to me now that I could easily see she was wearing an abbreviated cloth affair like a sarong cut off at the thighs. She had a lot of thick, black hair hanging loose down her back, and her lips pouted and her breasts pouted and her hips crowded the sarong, and I like crowds.

The orchestra played softly in the background, lowdown dirty rhythm with muted brass and brushes on the snare drum, and suddenly I recognized the number. I hadn't recognized it till now because I'd never heard it played like this before, but I'd always thought it was sensual as hell, particularly at the end. And it went well with the act, because it was Manuel de Falla's "Ritual Fire Dance."

Now I could hear Lorraine's bare feet slithering and slapping on the floor. She slipped out of the sarong, twisting and writhing, her shoulders shaking, and I don't know how I happened to notice, but she was smiling as if she were having a hell of a good time. Then she raised up on her toes with her arms stretched over her head and stood like that for a moment, wearing nothing but a heavy cloth brassiere and a wispy, flesh-colored G string, and the orchestra muttered in the background as the spotlight went out.

I thought, What the bloody hell? That was good, but was it all? The dance seemed awfully short, and the props had looked like a lot of trouble for so brief a number. Besides, that heavy bra hadn't seemed to go with the wispy G string.

Then, suddenly and with an audible hissing roar, those little flames behind her became torches that leaped up into the air and flared and flickered redly over the great painted idol and the body of the girl. Sweet Lorraine was still there, and now I knew: That heavy brassiere *didn't* go with the wispy G string.

She was still in the same position as when the spotlight had winked out, up on her toes and with her arms stretched above her head, but she'd traded that heavy cloth for a negligible sprinkling of some flecks of metallic powder that glistened on the jutting tips of her breasts like golden dust. She was motionless for only a moment, with the sound of the pulse-quickening music swelling up behind her and the torches' red flames leaping upward and sending shadows rippling over her white flesh, and then she swayed her shoulders gently from side to side and her breasts gleamed dully as they moved through the red glow that was the only illumination.

I don't know if she was still smiling or not; that's not where I was looking. And I wasn't smiling. I was jamming my teeth together. Then she really went into her dance and I forgot I was in the Pelican Club on the outskirts of Los Angeles, forgot I was starting a new case, forgot everything except the wild woman on the dance floor a few feet from me.

Because she was a wild woman: a wild, wild woman who twisted and turned and arched her body in a dance that gradually lost its gracefulness and became a savage, naked blending of throbbing music and writhing flesh and licking tongues of flame. It was no longer a graceful succession of movements liquidly flowing one into the other, but a frantic, frenetic series of shocks, each more violent than the last, an assault upon the flesh and a rape of the senses. This was a gift of woman, not a surrender, and the flames followed her as she

3

sank slowly to the floor, straining her body, quivering, her breasts shaking. Then she was lying on her back, her arms pressed flat against the polished wood, palms down, hips thrust into the air above her, writhing and jerking spasmodically. Suddenly the flames spurted higher into the air behind her and the music shrieked a minor discord as she tensed and held her rounded body motionless for long seconds, her hips thrust high off the floor. Then slowly she sank down, relaxed, as if exhausted. She lay still in the perfect quiet of the night club as the instruments of the orchestra sighed and gasped into silence, then the flames were suddenly snuffed out and the room was dark.

The darkness was complete for a moment, and there wasn't much applause. Probably everybody was too weak to use up that much more energy. I'm six-two and 205 pounds with practically no fat, and I was too weak. When the lights came back on the props were gone and the dancer was gone. I was gone, too, but I still sat gripping my highball glass. It was practically full. I emptied it.

So this, I was thinking, was Lorraine, the woman I'd come here to make conversation with. I was also thinking that I shouldn't have any trouble getting the information I wanted from her. Because Lorraine had already impressed me as a gal who, if she had any secrets, didn't want to keep them.

I sighed. All this had started because J. Harrison Bing wanted me to find his daughter, and if the case stayed as pleasant as this I was going to hate taking his money. I'd be willing to work for nothing except expenses, but Lorraine looked pretty expensive.

The place was starting to come to life again now that the floor show was over. The Pelican seated about two hundred customers, and almost all of the tables were occupied. People were dressed every which way, because this was Southern California, the early morning of May 10, 1951, and it was fairly warm. I noticed that most of the ringside tables were filled with older parties, and of the four men split two and two at tables on each side of me, three were bald. I felt a little out of place. First of all, I'm not old, I'm thirty; and I'm not bald in the slightest, though my inch-long hair is so nearly white that it has on at least one occasion fooled people into thinking so. It's real hair, though, and it's my own, as are the eyebrows that slant up at an angle over my gray eyes and then flop down at the corners in such a peculiar fashion that I've been accused of buying them in a joke shop.

The orchestra started playing "Be My Love," and a few couples drifted onto the dance floor. Their sedate swoops looked mighty dull after Lorraine's gyrations—and that reminded me. I caught the waiter's eye and he came over. I got out one of my cards that have "Sheldon Scott, Investigations" printed on them with the address of my office in the Hamilton Building in downtown Los Angeles. On the back of it I wrote, "I'd like to talk to you about Isabel

Ellis and William Carter for a few minutes. O.K.? Incidentally, would you care to go dancing?" I signed it "Shell Scott," wrapped the card in two one-dollar bills, and handed it to the waiter. I asked him if he'd give the card to the dancer and bring me her reply.

He looked at the two dollars and raised an eyebrow.

"Give her the *card*," I said.

"Yes, sir. To Miss Lorraine."

"Uh-huh. That's her real name?"

He hesitated, then apparently decided that this might be included for the paltry two dollars. "The dancer is Lorraine Mandel, sir. She is known professionally as Sweet Lorraine." And that was all of my money's worth because he wheeled around and marched off past the bandstand and through black draperies covering a doorway in the wall.

While I waited impatiently for my reply, I put my cards back into my wallet, together with the card my client had given me. It was a business card like my own, except that it was printed with "J. Harrison Bing," and Bing had crossed out the printed phone number with pencil and written in another number where he'd said I could reach him. I almost went to the phone and called him just to thank him for sending me to the Pelican. Imagine. He was paying me for this. And paying rather well, at that: $50 a day plus $1,000 bonus if I was successful in finding one Isabel Mary Ellis, his daughter, who had mysteriously disappeared.

I'd been settled down in my Hollywood apartment with a highball and Henry Miller's "Air-Conditioned Nightmare" when he'd shown up about ten P.M., three hours or so back, and introduced himself. He was a short, thin man who blinked mild blue eyes at me from under sparse eyebrows as he talked, and I guessed his age at close to sixty, though he could have been anywhere from around fifty on up. He explained that although he didn't hear from his daughter regularly, he'd had no word from her since before the first of the year, and letters he'd recently written her had come back unopened. Worried, he went from his Inglewood home to Isabel's home in L.A., only to find that she'd not only sold the house but disappeared bag and baggage, leaving no trace. Bing had made this discovery on May 3, less than a week ago. Really worried, he had on the following day retained a Los Angeles private detective named William Carter to find his daughter. Three nights later Carter phoned Bing and told him he'd got a good lead from a dancer named Lorraine at the Pelican Club, where Bing said Isabel had last worked as a cigarette girl. The next day Carter phoned Bing from the Desert Inn in Las Vegas, Nevada, and said the case was about wrapped up and that he was going to see a guy named Dante that night and would phone Bing again on the following day. Bing, on edge and worried sick, made Carter promise positively

5

to phone no matter what developed—and there'd been not a peep since out of Carter. It hadn't sounded especially serious to me, but Bing had been ready to throw a fit and had come to see me. So here I was, getting ready to talk to what Bing had described as "some kind of a dancer."

My waiter had been gone for no more than half a minute, and now he came back and walked up to my table. I couldn't think of any reason for it, but I got the impression he was nervous. Or maybe scared about something. He said, "I'm sorry, sir. She doesn't care to see you."

I frowned. "You gave her the card?"

"Why—yes, sir, of course."

Maybe I'd been a little too heavy-handed on that request to go dancing. Possibly her sense of humor was less elastic than she was. I asked the waiter, "She give you any reason?"

"None, sir."

This wasn't so good. I got out my wallet again. "How about trying once more, if you will. Tell her it's—"

He was already shaking his head, and his hand was palm out toward the wallet. First time I'd ever seen a waiter make that gesture. He said, "No, I. . . should rather not." Then he turned around and beat it.

I blinked after him. He hadn't even asked me if I cared for another drink. Well, the hell with him. I had only two leads to Isabel Ellis, my client's missing daughter, and Lorraine was one of them. While I was here I was at least going to make an honest effort to see her. I've been private-eyeing in and around Los Angeles for five years—ever since my discharge from the Marines after one of the wars—and I knew it was no time to give up when the gal herself hadn't yet told me to get lost. And that waiter had acted like no ordinary waiter.

I got up and walked past the bandstand and through the drapes my waiter had gone through a minute ago. Beyond them was a hall running left and right across the back of the Pelican, dimly illuminated by small, naked light bulbs. Three or four doors were set into the opposite wall, and a tall guy in a brown gabardine sports jacket was leaning against one of the doors.

I walked up to him and he grinned at me. He had white, too large teeth behind full lips, and deep brown eyes that were staring at me now.

I asked him, "This Lorraine's dressing room?"

He nodded, waving a mass of dry brown hair that needed some oil. It stuck up in the air like weeds and swelled out above each temple as if his brain were bulging out. I felt pretty sure that wasn't the reason. He leaned directly back against the door, facing me, and his heavy shoulders almost covered the entrance from one side to the other.

I said, pleasantly, "How about moving?"

He grunted and said, "I. . . don't think so," holding the "I" softly for three seconds, then squirting the rest out.

The silly grin on his face, and the wrong answer, and the *way* he'd answered started griping me a little. "Look, friend," I said. "I'd like to knock on the door. I'd hate to knock right through you."

He chuckled and moved aside. He walked a little way down the hall and looked back at me. "Come here," he said, as if he were going to tell me a secret. "Come on." He walked toward the entrance into the club and waved his hand for me to follow. I didn't get this guy. He paused in the doorway, waved again, and said, "Come on. I'll tell you something. You'll love this."

I walked up behind him and followed him into the club. He was a big guy, about an inch shorter than I, but his shoulders were even wider than mine. I was sizing him up, but it didn't seem necessary. He was acting like a man who had played with his brain too long. That's the impression I got then, which shows how wrong I can be.

Just inside the main room of the club he stopped and asked me, "You're Scott?"

"Yeah. How the hell did you know?" I'm easy to pick out because of my hair and eyebrows and size, and because of a slightly bent nose, but it seemed obvious that he must have seen the card I'd sent back with the waiter. He proved that deduction was correct by pulling the card out of the breast pocket of his coat, tearing the card in two, and handing me the pieces. He didn't explain that, just kept grinning and asked, "Where's your table, Scott?"

I didn't cotton to this boy, but I went along. I'll always go along so far. We weren't yet up to the point where I quit. I nodded toward the little table and he went over and climbed into the extra chair. I walked up and he pointed to my chair. "Sit down, Scott."

"The hell you say, mister. What kind of an act is this? What do you think you're pulling?"

"Not your leg, Scott," he said jovially. "Oh, come on. Sit down for a minute. Want to talk to you."

I sat down. I still couldn't figure the guy. He pushed the ash tray away from in front of him and leaned forward with his elbows on the table. I noticed a big vein that ran down the center of his forehead under the skin, bulging where the skin should have been smooth. I'm pretty brown from the sun, myself, but this guy was a deep bronze. He spent a lot of time in the sunshine.

He grinned and said, "You stay right here, now."

"What?"

"You heard me." His voice was pleasant. "You don't want to see Lorraine."

"Who the hell are you? I intend to see her as soon as you finish this conversation."

7

"Shut your face, Scott. And keep it shut." He said it casually, but my mouth dropped open.

I stared at him for five seconds. "You can't possibly be serious."

"Sure I'm serious." He went on in a singsong patter that was as light and frothy as soapsuds, but the words weren't light. "She doesn't want to see you, Scott. She's tired. You stay here, or better, you run along home. So you're Scott? Well. I've heard a little about you. Not much. Nothing good. Private eye, huh? That's funny. That's sure a laugh, pal. Yes, sir, you stay away from Lorraine. Otherwise I'll have to beat the water out of you, beat you half to death. I might even half kill you, Scott. No, that's wrong. Might kill you."

He kept going like that in a soft voice that must have sounded like droning conversation or a monologue to people at the next table, but he kept building it up and telling me with a kind of relish what he'd do to me if I didn't go home like a nice little boy. Finally he said a couple of things about my sexual habits that made up my mind fast while I looked around the club to see how many people would notice if I killed this bastard right here.

I said, "Hold it, pal. Just quiet down a minute." I stood up fast and started back toward the dressing room. The orchestra was having a short intermission, so I went straight across the dance floor and was halfway across before he scrambled out of the chair. I stopped and waited for him.

He came up beside me and the smile was gone for the first time. "Don't get excited," I said. "You've got the wrong idea." I grinned at him. He started to reach for me, then looked around, and I went on ahead through the black drapes. He was a little confused now, just as I'd been, and two yards inside the hallway I stopped and turned around and said to him as he came up close, "Look, you don't understand. I'm sorry as hell about all this—" and cut it off while he was staring at me. I was looking right at him as pleasantly as I could with all that burn in me, and I reached up fast with both hands crossed at the wrist, my right hand going to my left and grabbing the lapel of his gabardine jacket while my left hand crossed over and got the lapel on the other side, my thumbs out and my fingers on the inside of his coat, and before he could even get his hands up I tightened my grip and scissored my arms outward hard, and my wrists ground into his neck

He didn't have a chance. He'd barely started to grab my wrists, but he couldn't do a damn thing about it because he was unconscious in no more than two short seconds, and I gave him a final squeeze as he sagged, then I dropped him.

I left him there and turned around and walked to the door of the dressing room. I was still so damned mad I didn't even knock, just slammed open the door and went in.

2

I DON'T know what I expected to find in there after the warning old unconscious had just given me. Maybe I expected a dead body.

There was a body, all right, but it was about the least dead body I'd seen lately: Lorraine, Sweet Lorraine, and she looked up in surprise as I came bursting in.

She was sitting before a dressing table ringed with open light bulbs, wearing a yellow dressing gown that was too old for so young a lady, and she should have thrown it away, and she could throw it away any time she felt like it as far as I was concerned. And I was getting concerned. Close up, her face was cuter than it had appeared on the dance floor. She had impudent eyes and lips and a little button of a nose that wasn't quite big enough for the full lips that looked willing and big blue eyes that looked wise. I would have enjoyed talking to her immensely, only she wasn't alone.

In a chair on her left was a man who also looked up when I came in. There wasn't surprise on his face so much as a cold kind of fury, and in the few seconds while we all said nothing, I looked him over good.

He was somewhere in his middle thirties. He looked prosperous and well fed, though he wasn't tall, but he also looked as if he'd come up in the world

9

the hard way and got tougher with every inch of the climb. There weren't any marks on his face that didn't look as if they'd been stamped there by time and ambition and maybe greed, but his face looked frozen, as if it had been dipped in liquid oxygen, and I got the crazy impression that if he smiled his face would crack and splinter like the animated-cartoon characters that jump into empty swimming pools.

Not that there was anything Donald Duckish about him. If he looked like any kind of animal other than man, it was like a predatory bird: a hawk. Primarily because of his eyes and nose. The nose was pinched in at the nostrils, making him look like a man with a head cold sucking for air, and his eyes were small and dark. But the small eyes were set far apart in his face so that the proportions didn't seem exactly right. It was almost as if he were looking at me from opposite sides of his brain, sizing me up.

And I guess he was sizing me up, but he did it fast, because shortly after I stepped into the dressing room he swore at me like a man who'd decided my ancestry in five seconds. It took him about that long; he stared at me when I came in the door, and that hard face seemed to congeal for a breath, then he pulled his mouth open like a man doing it from memory and said, "You son of a bitch."

What the hell was everybody so mad at me for? I thought about choking this one, too, for a minute, but though I was still so griped I could hardly think straight, I ignored him for the moment and turned to the girl.

She said, "What are you doing in here?" She sounded just as she looked: surprised.

I said, "I sent you a note saying I wanted to talk to you. Didn't you get it?"

She shook her head. "No. What note? What for?"

"It was on my card. You worked with Isabel Ellis. I want to talk to you about her. Privately, if you don't mind." I calmed down a bit, remembering this was her dressing room and that I'd just barged in. I said, "I'm sorry about busting in this way, but I had a little trouble outside. I—got steamed up."

She shook her head. "But I don't even know any Isabel Ellis."

That stopped me. I said, "Huh?" I started to add some more, then looked at the frozen-faced guy who was still glaring at me. He glanced at the girl, and she said to me, "It's all right. Go on."

My head was still spinning. I said, "You don't know her? Maybe you knew her as Isabel Bing; that was her maiden name." She looked blank, and I asked her, "You know a detective named William Carter, though, don't you?"

She shook her head again. I was going around in circles. I asked her, "Can we go over this in private? It won't take more than a few minutes."

She didn't need to answer. The hawk-faced guy got up and gave me one last glare, looking as if he were ready to split down the middle, then stalked out. I wondered who he was and what he was doing here, but then I stopped wondering because I remembered my singsong friend lying in the hall right where he could step on him as he walked out. And I remembered that this call was supposed to be such a simple thing that I hadn't carried along my revolver. Perhaps I should have checked the fellow I'd choked and made sure he didn't have a gun. People hardly ever carry guns, at least nice people don't, but then, he hadn't been a nice person.

I said to Lorraine, "Look, I apologize for throwing my weight around your room, but I've got to get some information. And I—can't stay long. How about this Isabel?"

"I told you I don't know her."

"She worked with you here a few months ago. Cigarette girl."

She just looked blank some more. Then she said, "I don't even know who *you* are."

She was right. "I forgot you didn't get my card," I said. "My name's Shell Scott. I'm a private detective. Look, I'll make this fast. A couple of nights ago another private detective, a guy named William Carter, came here and talked to you. He wanted the same information I do. What you know about Isabel Ellis, and where she went from here. It was my impression that you told him and that he followed whatever lead you gave him—and he went from here straight to Las Vegas, Nevada. What about that?"

"Nothing about it. There's nothing to it. I don't know what you're talking about."

"You are Lorraine Mandel, aren't you?"

"Yes."

And that was the end of the conversation. That was very nearly the end of everything. Because behind me a voice said, "That's enough for now, Scott, so shut your face and let's go," and it was said in a singsong and I knew he had a gun before I even turned around. I was right.

I went peacefully into the hall and the guy pulled the door shut, making sure I wasn't close to him when he did it. He was wearing his big-toothed smile, but it looked tired. He said, "I told you what I'd do to you, Scott."

"I could have choked you a little longer, friend."

"Might be you should have. You better listen to me good this time, Scott. You stand right there for a minute, then you do what I say, and you listen good now." He paused a second or two, then said slowly, no singsong, "Stay clear the hell away from Vegas. You got that? You don't, and you'll get killed. Killed for sure, all the way dead. And forget this Carter crap. Forget Carter,

11

forget Vegas, forget Lorraine, forget me. It's a promise: If you don't forget good, you'll get killed by somebody."

He didn't say who would kill me, but that seemed relatively unimportant. But, also, he hadn't once mentioned any Isabel Ellis, and I thought that neglect might someday be important if I lived. And, right at this moment especially, I wanted to live. I wanted to live to be an old, old man.

"Go on, move," he said. "Out that way. Straight ahead."

Straight ahead was the end of the hallway. The hallway ran parallel to the street that fronted the club, so that open door ahead of me probably led into the darkness of an alley. I didn't like going out there, but the guy with the gun behind me was just far enough away so I couldn't get close to him, and close enough so he couldn't miss. I started walking, moving as slowly as I could, while the bushy-haired boy behind me talked and told me positively and definitely all over again what I was not supposed to do.

Then he said, "Just to make sure you don't forget, Scott, I'm going to give you something to remember it by." He said it all in the same patter, but the tone of his voice wasn't light at all and I knew if ever anybody meant what he said, this boy did.

I had a reasonably clear idea of what he meant by now, but that last bit hadn't sounded as if he intended to put a bullet in me, and I was getting ready to take off as soon as I hit that open door. My head was still buzzing with what had happened in this last half hour and I was wondering where the frozen-faced guy had gone. I didn't really expect to find out, but just as I tensed my muscles to jump and stepped through the door into the darkness beyond, I did find out. The hard way.

Light glinted on something in the alley on my left, and by the time I saw it was reflection on a car's chrome it was too late and I'd swung my head to the left. Wrong way.

Whatever it was that slammed against the back of my skull was solid, and it was heavy, but it didn't put me completely out. Right from the beginning I wished it had, because then I wouldn't have felt the asphalt paving slam into my face, or the shoes in my ribs, or the next crashing blow on the side of my skull, and the darkness would have swallowed me up even sooner than it finally did.

But at least I found out there were two of them for sure, because no one guy could have slugged and kicked me in so many different places in so short a time.

3

I SAT in the darkness of the alley, with the stench of garbage clogging my nostrils, and held my head while anger simmered inside me and grew bigger and hotter. Finally, though, I squeezed it down inside me out of the way for now. But I know it was still there, ready to flare up when the time came.

After a few minutes or half an hour I felt better. I thought that if I worked real hard at it I could move. Another case was starting out with bumps and bangs, and the bumps had been O.K. but the bangs had been on the top of my head. I pulled myself over toward the wall and my hand sank into something squishy on the asphalt, and for one horrible moment I thought it was part of me. That's how I found out the bastards had not only left me lying unconscious and half dead, but had turned the garbage barrel upside down over me. Even without that I'd have remembered them.

When the ringing died down inside my head I slid over to the wall and eased up against the rough brick, remembering that all the time I'd talked to J. Harrison Bing earlier this evening I'd had the feeling he wasn't telling me all he should or could. I'd even mentioned it to him, but he'd sworn he'd told me everything of the slightest importance.

That's what the man had said. But now I sat in this goddamned alley with my head spinning because I didn't know what the hell the score was and also because my head had been severely pounded, and I didn't know a thing for sure except that already in this screwy case something smelled even worse than the stinking garbage.

I looked at my watch and saw it was already after two A.M. and the club was closed. I hobbled around, though, and banged on the doors to get in, but it was no soap. I didn't know where Lorraine was or where I could find her tonight, so I headed back toward my apartment thinking that I'd see about Sweet Lorraine in the morning even though the way I felt now I didn't know if I'd last that long. As I tooled my antique yellow Cadillac back toward Hollywood I couldn't help thinking that I was the boy who'd wanted to live to be an old, old man. Well, now I'd made it.

Dr. Paul Anson, whose apartment is two doors from my three rooms and bath on the second floor of the Spartan Apartment Hotel, said, "Next time get killed; I've got an operation tomorrow," grinned at me, and shut the door in my face. He'd just finished looking me over and it appeared that I was relatively whole and would live after all. I walked down to my apartment and let myself in.

Inside I stopped long enough to feed the tropical fish I keep in two aquariums just inside the door, then I went into the kitchenette and mixed a stiff drink, poured half of it down my throat, and went back into the front room. I lay down flat on my back on the oversized chocolate-brown divan, grabbed the phone, and plopped it down on my stomach.

Now that I'd had time to relax and slow down a bit I realized that although I had a score to settle with the frozen-faced guy and a singsonging jerk, that part was personal and should come after the job. And my one and only job was to find Isabel Ellis, so I dialed the operator and put in a long-distance call to Wilbur Clark's Desert Inn in Las Vegas. Before this went any further I wanted to be sure Detective William Carter wasn't up there getting sloppy at the bar.

I got the room clerk at the desk of the Desert Inn. Even over the phone I could sense the color and lights and gaiety that I remembered from two previous trips to Las Vegas, and I could almost hear the ivory ball rolling around the rims of the roulette wheels, and the whir of the slot machines. Just imagining it was so pleasant that the anger still with me faded a bit and I felt better.

But that was the only part that made me feel better. I learned that Carter hadn't used his room at all and couldn't be reached. After futilely having him paged I asked the clerk, "He hasn't checked out, then?"

"No. We're holding his bill. He came in on the eighth, as you said, for an indefinite stay."

14

That was about as much as I could get on the phone. "O.K., thanks a lot. Now, I'll be in Las Vegas tomorrow—or, rather, later today—probably in the afternoon. I'd like to make a reservation for about—"

He cut in, "I'm sorry, sir. There are no vacancies."

"Huh? This is Thursday morning, isn't it? I thought—"

"I'm afraid that almost everything in town will be taken, sir. This is the beginning of Helldorado Week. May tenth through May thirteenth, sir. Thursday through Sunday, inclusive."

That was all he needed to say. Helldorado. The wildest, shootingest, root-ing-tootingest ruckus since the West was really wild; the biggest thing since MacArthur's arrival in New York. Four days when Las Vegas, which jumps plen-ty all the year around, jumps clear up into the air and clicks its spurred heels. I had as much chance of getting a good room as I had of waking up in the morn-ing with no bruises.

I thought a minute, remembering the guys I knew in Vegas. I'd bumped into plenty, but there was only one I could think of right away who was actu-ally a good friend. I said, "Say, you still got a young bartender there named Freddy Powell?"

The clerk's voice got less impersonal right away. "Sure. You know Freddy?" Then he must have remembered the foolish dictum not to get chummy with cus-tomers, and added, "However, he works days, sir. He's been off since six o'clock."

"Any chance he's still around? If I remember Freddy, he might still be at the bar."

I heard him chuckle. "Yes, indeed, sir. I'll have him paged. Even if he is here, it may take a while."

"Yeah," I said, "I know." I gave the clerk my number and asked him to have Freddy phone me if he was present and conscious. I added, "Tell him it's Shell Scott," then I put the phone on the carpet and relaxed. Freddy Powell might not be at the Desert Inn, but wherever he was, I'd have made book he was doing one of three things: sitting somewhere with a highball or a bottle, in bed with a woman, or bending some blonde's ear. He was a bastard, but he was sure an interesting bastard.

I met him on my first trip to Las Vegas, where I'd wound up after locating a witness in Boulder City. Freddy was tending bar downtown then and we got to talking across the mahogany. He gave me a couple of drinks on the house, then I bought him a drink and he gave me another on the house. We took off together when his shift ended, two hours later, and from then on things got a bit fuzzy. But we'd had such a rip-roaring time together that my next trip to Vegas was a vacation trip motivated as much by a desire to see Freddy again as by the fact that Vegas is a hell of a town. I was still thinking about that second trip—fuzzier even than the first one—when the phone rang. I picked it up.

15

"Hello, Shell? That you, Shell? Hi, you old satyr, you. What's up, and don't answer that. Say hello to Shell, Angel. Hey, Shell, this is Angel."

I hadn't got a word in yet For all he knew, he was talking to the janitor. Then another voice, a low, soft, feminine voice, rustled over the phone, "Hello, Shell," it said, and all of a sudden I wanted to go to Vegas whether I was on a job or not.

I said, "Well, hello. Tell me, are you a blonde?"

And Freddy said, "You think she's listening? Think I'm gonna let you at her? No, sir. How are you?"

"Freddy," I said, "you've been drinking." It was five minutes before we got around to my reason for calling him, but finally I told him, "Look, chum, since I'm coming up sometime today, I'll need a room. I forgot about Helldorado starting. Can you fix me up with a place to sleep?"

"Just a minute," he said. "I'll ask Angel." He was gone for a moment, then, "No good. She's leaving in the morning. They'll sure as hell have her room rented, too. I'll do what I can, though. If I can't find something good you can have my room."

The unique thing about his last sentence was that he meant exactly what he'd said. He was that kind of guy. Whatever he could do for anybody he liked, he'd do without thinking twice about it. I told him not to wear himself out and added, "Something else. I'm coming up to look for a gal named Isabel Ellis, and I'll try to hunt up a private detective named William Carter. This Carter registered there at the Desert Inn but nobody can find the guy now. How about nosing around a little when you sober up? If he's there, maybe I can take a vacation and we'll hang another one on."

"Sure thing," he said. "Sounds good. See you tomorrow, huh?"

"Yeah. Say good-by to Angel for me."

He chuckled happily. "Sure, pal. I'll have one for you."

I hung up on him. If I hadn't had several things to check here in L.A. in the morning, I'd have leaped in the Cad and been on my way.

But instead I finished my drink and went to bed and dreamed of a little roulette wheel with a white ivory ball rolling around in the groove at the top, but when I looked closer I saw it wasn't a white ball at all but a tiny naked blonde, and she was running like hell because there, loping along behind her and right in the groove, was Freddy.

16

4

THE first thing I did in the morning after a hot shower, which didn't take enough of the ache out of my bones, and a quick toast-and-coffee breakfast was to stop at the desk on my way out. My new client hadn't had a picture of his daughter with him last night, but he'd assured me he'd bring me one or leave one at the desk. He had. I picked up the picture and looked at it, remembering Bing's description of his daughter: five-two, 110 pounds or so, twenty-nine years old, dark hair, blue eyes. It could have been a million women. In the photo, though, Isabel Ellis was a pretty little gal with big eyes and dark hair worn in an upsweep, a short upper lip, and a pleasant smile. The portrait, a black-and-white eight-by-ten, was clear and maybe it would help. I put it in my bag with the rest of my stuff and took off for the legwork I had to take care of before I started for Las Vegas.

Bing had also told me that his daughter had been married to one Harvey Ellis here in Los Angeles, and that though they weren't divorced, they were separated. Harvey Ellis had left Isabel, Bing told me, just up and deserted her, and he'd seemed so embarrassed by the intimate details that I didn't press it. He did tell me that he had no idea where Ellis was. I drove to 220 North Broadway and went into the Hall of Records, took a look at the file copies of the marriage application and certificate of Harvey Ellis and Isabel Bing, and put in a rush order for photostats. I learned by asking around that I was the second man to get the info in the past week. Carter's stock went up a little with me, because it's surprising how many private detectives themselves fail to realize how much information of benefit in a missing-persons investigation the marriage file contains.

While I was near the City Hall I paid a brief visit to Homicide, not because I had business there, but to ask help of my good friend Phil Samson, the Homicide captain. I gave him a cigar and the dope on Harvey Ellis I'd copied down at the Hall of Records, and promised him another cigar if he checked a little on Harvey and wired any information he got to me at the Desert Inn. For all I knew, wifey might have gone back to hubby. Luckily I've known Sam for years, worked with him and even broken some cases for him—with his help—so all he did was get blue in the face and swear at me as usual. But before I left he told me he'd check, and also check the morgue and Missing Persons, and it would cost me not a cigar, but a box of Corona Grandes.

I left City Hall and checked the house that Isabel had sold, and learned that it had been in her name and had been sold through a real-estate agency for cash on December 6, on which day Isabel had picked up the money and left. That was just before the first of the year—and Bing hadn't heard from his daughter since the first of the year.

Next I checked William Carter in the phone book and went to his house, where I talked with Mrs. Carter. She was a pleasant little woman with a sweet voice, and she told me over the squalling of a baby in the background that she hadn't heard from Willie in a couple of days but that she wasn't worried because often he'd get tied up on a job for a week or so at a time. I did get a look at a hand-colored studio portrait of him, though: a red-haired guy about thirty-five, with a thick red mustache and an old jagged scar over his left eye.

Everything so far had been routine, so I spent a half hour finding out where Lorraine Mandel lived, went to her hotel, and got the first big, fat shock. She'd joined the act. I wouldn't be talking to Lorraine this morning.

The landlady, a thin, bony woman of about fifty, came to the door of the office when I knocked. I said, "Good morning. I'd like to see Miss Mandel, if I may."

"Oh," she said, "she's not here any more. She moved."

I stared at her. "Moved? You mean left? She's not here?"

"No, she just left this morning. I'm sorry."

I almost said, "You're sorry!" but I held my tongue and started easing questions into her. And, finally, as usual, money talked louder than I did. For a twenty-dollar bill she finally said, "Well, she asked me not to tell. I really shouldn't say anything."

I grinned at her, rather a strained grin. She already had my twenty stuffed down the front of her dress. "You do know where she is, though."

"Well, not exactly. She told me where to forward her mail, is all. But I wasn't supposed to say. . . Well, she said to send it up to that new night club. Place called The Inferno, she said. In Las Vegas."

"Las Vegas?"

"Las Vegas."

She'd said Las Vegas, all right. That town was popping up too much in this case for comfort. My comfort. That was all that the landlady could tell me, so I left. I stopped at the Hall of Records and picked up my photostats, still thinking about the landlady. What she'd told me seemed pretty poor information for twenty dollars when I might have got it for nothing at the post office if Lorraine had put in for a change of address. And then one little brain cell exploded. I was back in the Cadillac and driving down First Street when I remembered that J. Harrison Bing had repeated for me something that Detective William Carter had said. As far as I knew, they were Carter's last words, too. Carter had said, "I'm going out to Dante's place tonight." And Lorraine's mail was to be forwarded to The Inferno. I juggled it, but there was only one answer. Inferno—Dante: Dante's Inferno.

And with that little thought shivering in my brain, I tromped on the gas and headed, not too gaily, for Las Vegas, Nevada, and the Lord knew what.

The road slanted downward from the hills behind me and stretched rigidly ahead through shimmering desert as dry as a dead man's bones. I couldn't help thinking in terms of dead men, because in less than an hour I'd be rolling down the Strip in Las Vegas, and I had the growing feeling that at least one dead man might already lie somewhere up there ahead of me, and maybe one dead woman, and I remembered, too, a singsong voice in my ear last night telling me to stay away from Las Vegas unless I liked dying.

I pushed the old Cadillac up to seventy-five crossing the barren, cracked earth at the California-Nevada border, and she purred along like a two-ton tiger. The Cad's an old '41, and she's a sort of hideous yellow, but she's got power under the hood and responds to every touch of my hand like the wise old lady she is. I've got a deep and abiding affection for two inanimate things: my Cad and my gun. On that first business trip to Boulder City I'd got a permit to carry a gun in the state of Nevada, so now my short-barreled .38 Colt Special, with five cartridges in the cylinder and an empty chamber under the hammer, nestled comfortingly in the holster at my left shoulder. It was a comfort to me, but if anyone else got ideas about sapping me, it wasn't going to be a comfort to him.

This was the afternoon of May tenth, the first day of Helldorado, and I was bruised and tired. My head ached and my hands tingled from the hours

19

of steady driving from L.A., but I was keyed up and I had to tell myself to relax, take it easy, save my energy for what might be coming later.

It was coming sooner than I thought. A few minutes before five P.M., when I was ten miles from downtown Las Vegas, things started happening. It wasn't going to be until later in the evening that I'd be sure they were happening the wrong way for me, but I was just jittery enough to play it extra-safe. And maybe that saved my life.

It started with a robin's-egg-blue Chrysler sedan, the big 1951 New Yorker model. I didn't pay much attention to it except to note that it was pretty and that it was coming from Las Vegas. It whooshed by me going in the opposite direction, and I wouldn't have thought any more about it except that the two men in it craned their necks at me or at my too damned distinctive Cadillac as they went by. But I caught them in the rear-view mirror as their car slowed, swung around fast in the middle of the road, and came roaring like a singed bat out of hell after me.

I was still hitting a good seventy, but the big Chrysler must have been pushing a hundred because it was rapidly looming larger in the mirror, and I knew I was being too jittery and that these boys might only be going back to town because they'd remembered some unfinished business; but I couldn't help thinking, in view of what had happened to me lately, that maybe that unfinished business was me. So I pulled my .38 out of its holster and held it ready in my lap, steering with my left hand. The Chrysler came up fast and I slacked off on the accelerator a little. As I slowed down they swung out on the left to pass and I lifted my foot off the gas ready for the quickest stop in the Cad's history if the boys alongside had guns or tried to crowd me off the road.

Because they were alongside now. There were two of them, the driver and the one on this side, and they didn't have any guns but they were sure grabbing an eyeful of me. I had the .38 out of sight but pointed in the proper direction to put a hole in the nearest guy's face, but they just slowed down as I slowed down, right alongside, got their big fat look, then zoomed away from me as if I were parked.

I didn't know what that meant except that those guys weren't casual sightseers and that they'd scared me. They'd taken a good look at me, but I'd had just as good a look at them, and I wouldn't forget them. Not ever. Not, at least, for the rest of my life.

The blue Chrysler was almost out of sight. They must have been very nearly into town, and right now I was prejudiced against driving boldly into Vegas after them. I knew, when I decided to drive up, that if anybody wanted to spot me, he could do it—even if he didn't know me—with one look at my car if he had seen it before or even heard what it looked like. I couldn't think of any other reason for those two boys to stare at me; I'd never seen either of them before.

Now I almost wished I'd flown up, but I'd checked the plane times before I left and figured by pushing the Cad I could get here as soon as the plane. And that gave me an idea. I glanced at my watch and noted that it was five o'clock, ten minutes before the arrival time of the next L.A. plane. And I could see the airport now. McCarran Field is about five hundred yards off the road on the right of U.S. Highway 91, and two or three miles before you reach the Flamingo, the first club on the Las Vegas Strip. I turned in at the airport road, drove in, and parked around at the right of the long, low building that houses the offices and soda fountain.

I sat smoking part of a cigarette and decided that my best approach would be money. Then I put the car keys in my coat pocket, got out of the car, and walked inside the building. It took me five minutes of the ten remaining before the plane arrived, but I finally spotted the young kid about twenty-two in the black chauffeur's cap. Otherwise he was dressed in ordinary civilian clothes. I walked up to him.

"Friend, how would you like to make a fast ten bucks?"

He had a pink face and bloodshot eyes, as if he were recovering from celebrating Helldorado early. He blinked at me and said, "What do I gotta do?"

"Nothing. No kidding, it isn't a gag. Come on outside."

He looked puzzled, but he followed me out to a spot where we wouldn't be overheard. I asked him, "You drive the limousine that takes the passengers into town? That black Packard out front?"

He nodded.

"Let's just say I've always wanted to drive a limousine. It's worth ten bucks. All you have to do is lend me your cap. And the limousine."

He blinked some more. "Jesus, mister, I can't do that."

"Why not? You'll get it back. I'll even deliver the plane passengers. Where do you take them?"

"Anyplace in town they want to go. But I can't. . . " He stopped, thinking, then shook his head. "I might get fired. I been thinking about quitting for Helldorado, but no sense getting *fired*."

"Hell, nobody'll even know about it. You can take a nap or something. Better than that, you can go along."

"I don't know," he said. "You could go in with me. Why you gotta *drive* the thing?"

If anyone were looking for me, I didn't think he'd expect me at the wheel of a black limousine. Besides, no matter what I was in, I wanted to be at the wheel just in case. "Well," I said, and stopped. We could hear the drone of twin engines now as the plane started coming in. "Because," I said quickly, "there's twenty-five bucks in it for you. You can put it on the red tonight."

"Twenty-five?" His eyes got a gleam in them and I added, "That's positively tops. I'll drive, drop off the passengers, then get out at the Desert Inn. You can drive straight back." He looked ready to weaken, so I said, "Oh, the hell with it," and turned around.

He said to my back, "O.K. Gimme the twenty-five." He sighed. "But look, if anybody asks what's wrong, tell them I suddenly got sick and you're helping me out." He sighed again. "I was gonna quit anyway."

I told him O.K., slipped him the money, and took the cap. Then I hustled over and got my bag out of the Cad and put it up front in the limousine, climbed behind the wheel, and put on the cap. The kid told me all I had to do was wait for the passengers to climb in, then take them where they were going. Another guy handled the baggage, he said, which would make it easier for me.

The plane came in, the passengers got off, and some of them straggled up to the limousine. I kept my face turned away in case any of them were old hands on this line and wanted to know what the score was. In about five minutes we were ready to go, with the kid sitting on my right on the front seat acting sick. I put the buggy in low and took off. This was easy. This was a breeze. I felt pretty good, but as we approached the Flamingo on the right, I saw the blue car just this side of it about ten feet back in the curving drive that swung in front of the ornate entrance of the club that "Bugsy" Siegel used to control. The Chrysler was facing out, ready to go, and one of the two men was standing beside the car looking out toward the highway. I swung my face away, around to the left, just as two things happened: I thought how cute it would be if somebody wanted out at the Flamingo, and a booming voice from the rear said, "I'd like out at the Flamingo."

I kept my head to the left as we passed the entrance to the big hotel, then turned it straight ahead as the voice boomed, a little angrily now, "Don't you hear? Stop. I say *stop!*"

I wasn't about to stop. I rolled right on by. The kid groaned sickly. I was past the first road block by now, and maybe there weren't any more, so I looked over my shoulder at the man with the big voice, who was big and sloppy-fat and about fifty, and said, "I'm sorry, sir, I'll drop you off on the way back. I'm new on—" and I busted it off in the middle when I saw Lorraine, Sweet Lorraine, eyeballing me with her chin damn near down to her gold dust.

I think I squeaked a little when I saw her sitting clear over on the right side of the back seat, but then it occurred to me that I should have known that if she were heading for Vegas she could well be on the plane, and I finished my sentence miserably: ". . . the. . . job."

I turned around to the front again with my brain a little numb, and decided that numb was its usual condition, and the Flamingo's loss shouted, "I want out now! *Now!* Aaaargh!" as the kid at my right groaned sickly and softly, "Oooh, the fat bastard," and then a tiny voice from the right of the rear seat said, "Let me out here," and I looked to the right of the road for my first glimpse of Dante's Inferno. Well, at least I'd seen the damned place.

I let Lorraine out along with two other people, then made the rounds till all were dropped off except the guy simmering in the back seat. Ever since I'd been so uncouth as to drive past the Flamingo so I wouldn't, perhaps, get killed, he'd been sitting back there muttering to himself and the other passengers about this-is-an-outrage-bloody-outrage-I'll-report-that-young-man and so on. He was all alone back there now, but still muttering. When I headed back up the Strip he said, "I'll report you."

"You'll report me, hell. I stole the damn car. I'm just going for a ride."

The kid chuckled happily, sympathizing with me, but the guy subsided for a moment. I don't think he believed me, though; I think he thought I was crazy. I had him pegged as one of those guys so full of his own importance that he could hardly stand it. He was so full of something else that I could hardly stand it. I've run into his type before. They think that anyone who chauffeurs a limousine or taxi, or waits table, or bellhops, is an animal on a par with the slug, and it gave me great pleasure to pull in at the Desert Inn and park in front of the entrance, trade the cap for my bag, and get out of the car. Fatty was sputtering as I got out of the car and he said, "What. . . what. . ." and the kid was almost hysterical with happiness.

I slammed the door and Fatty pushed out his lips, his jelly cheeks quivering, and he wiggled a pudgy finger at me. "You. . . you. . . I'll have you discharged. I *demand* that you drive me to the Flamingo!" His voice went up and up right along with his blood pressure.

I glanced at the kid and he was grinning, and I looked back at Fatty and said, "Mister, I just quit. And you can bloody well walk."

The car was still there and he was still in the back when I went into the Desert Inn. Possibly he'd had a stroke.

5

THE second set of inch-thick glass doors swung shut behind me and I took three steps inside and stopped. This was for me. This was wonderful. I remembered bits I'd read in the Kefauver Report, and in the Volstead Act, and it was still wonderful.

I was looking right out through the huge picture windows in the lobby's far wall at the Olympic-size figure-eight swimming pool being used by more women than you could shake at. On my left was the desk, and beyond it the hallway to the downstairs rooms and the stairway up to the second floor front, and straight ahead was the Cactus Room, and humming and buzzing on my right beyond the stairs to the Sky Room Cocktail Lounge was the twenty-four-hour-a-day casino. The whole inside of the hotel and the area around the pool was boiling with people.

Here in this mass of men and women there wasn't too much trouble that could come my way, but no matter if eighteen torpedoes were after me, the noise and life and gaiety looked so good to me that from here on out the Shell Scott motto was "Damn the torpedoes, full speed ahead."

And now, for the first time, I could really look at a little part of Las Vegas again. I was in the land of sunshine and desert and quickie divorces and gambling fever and nine thousand beautiful women and more. Now I could look at it and smell it and hear it. And now I could really tell it was Helldorado. Maybe I'd been too preoccupied up till this moment to notice, but here inside the doors of the most beautiful luxury hotel in Las Vegas—and one of the most beautiful anywhere, for my money—I couldn't miss it.

Helldorado: when a whole town goes pleasantly berserk for four days and uncounted thousands of people crowd into Las Vegas and jam together in the side-by-side gambling halls downtown or rub shoulders out here in the luxury hotels and casinos on the Strip; when a whole town stands on its head and does a Western can-can complete with brass bands and parades, beauty contests and world-championship rodeos, cowboys and real Indians, and beards and babes and bottles. It's a robust pioneer town, model 1951, with all the yahoo and yippee and red-eyed hallelujah of resurrected Tombstone and the Comstock and Custer's Last Stand, and thousands of crazy people live for four days with their boots on.

It's what they call the "Mardi Gras with pistols," a wild and wonderful town with, all day long and all night long, guns going off. . . Guns going off? *Guns* going off!

I wished I were back in Los Angeles.

But I was here, so I went on in. I pushed through the crowd in the lobby, about two out of ten of the people in some kind of Western costume, and right in front of me a cute little gal in a black-and-white cowgirl outfit of calfskin jacket and skirt stamped a little white boot and put another nickel in a slot machine. She looked up and smiled brightly at me, apparently for no other reason than that she felt good. I smiled back at her for no reason at all. I squeezed past her and into the lush casino. Till now all I'd heard was voices and the whir of slot machines, but in the big gaming room I could hear the dealers at roulette and dice tables calling the points and the numbers. On my right as I went in was the Lady Luck Bar, the "longest bar in Nevada," and behind it on the wall light was still flickering from number to number around the oversize roulette wheel, which meant that somebody seated at one of the matching numbers at the bar would wind up with a free silver dollar.

The place was so jammed that I didn't see Freddy right away, but I walked around the table of hot hors d'oeuvres and then between the cocktail tables on my left and the bar on my right, till almost at the end I spotted him.

I should have known. He was completely oblivious of all the hubbub around him, and was leaning forward talking to a woman seated at the far end of the Lady Luck Bar. I couldn't tell much about her except that she had a whole mass of hair piled high on top of her head. Even for me, that was almost too much hair. But if Freddy was all wrapped up in a fast conversation with her, she was probably choice enough. As I walked closer to them I

25

noticed a young guy pounding on the bar with a silver dollar, trying to get a drink out of Freddy. Freddy kept on talking.

He said something to the girl and she laughed, throwing back her head. It was a nice, healthy, honest laugh and I liked it. I was feeling better. I got clear up to the end and stopped about a foot from the girl, between her stool and the next one, which was also occupied. Freddy was going along a mile a minute, his blue eyes merry under straight, thick eyebrows as black as his crinkly hair. He had good strong teeth and you saw a lot of them because he was a happy kind of guy. And a damned good-looking guy.

I just stood there, and I hadn't paid much attention to the girl, but I looked at her as she took a cigarette out of her mouth, stuck out her tongue, and brushed at a stray bit of tobacco with the tip of a long red fingernail. Just as she flicked it away, she slanted her eyes over toward me. I was gawking at her, and her lips curved a little and her eyes wrinkled with the start of a smile.

I was dead.

She was beautiful, out of this world, wonderful. It hit me all in a rush, with no details right away, but only the first total impression of her, and I just stood there and looked. The wide-eyed innocence of a brand new Eve bloomed on her face, but it was on a body that had been improved through two billion years: a body that was sex boiled and distilled till only the essence was left. She had rust-red hair and soft brown eyes, and lips that were mobile and full and smooth, but I had to get back to that incredible body.

She was Woman, that's all, just sex on wheels in high gear and going downhill; no brakes and a hand on the horn. She wasn't in Western costume; she was dressed for afternoon cocktails in a black skirt and a wine-colored faille jacket worn outside the skirt and held with a wide golden belt. The collar of the jacket stood up behind her neck, with two little points like wings at each side of her head, and the front slanted down in a wide V, and her white breasts peeked out of the V as if anxious to get a good look, which also described me at the moment.

And she couldn't have been wearing a brassiere because there just wasn't room for it. She might have been wearing two Band-aids, but nothing much bigger than that. And right at those points in my pleasant conjectures she leaned way over, way to hell over, and stubbed out her cigarette, and in the wine-tinted shadow cast by her jacket as it fell forward away from her body I caught a curving flash of creamy white blending into a rosy sphere and I knew for sure she wasn't wearing Band-aids.

I was being rude and lecherous and not at all the little gentleman, and my only excuse was that I didn't even know it: I simply stood there like a dying man who had only that moment discovered that women were different. I just stood there and stood there and looked and looked.

She didn't seem to mind. She didn't seem to mind a bit. But finally she turned her head and looked at me and said in a soft, crackly voice that would take the sting out of anything and that went with the face, "Darn you, mister, you're making me nervous." But she didn't mean it, because her misty brown eyes didn't mean it and her lips were smiling, and because she took a deep breath and held it. It was just a sentence, a conversational gambit, and I said, "Hello, you're wonderful," and hoped that if I got killed on this trip it would wait at least till this night was over, wait at least till tomorrow, because she wasn't getting away from me, not this one.

I'd forgotten about Freddy, but then he yelped, "Shell!! Why, you old satyr, you. When'd you get in?"

I didn't look at him right away because I winced a little and kept watching the girl's face to see what that "satyr" would do to it. It didn't do anything. She didn't seem to have noticed.

Then I turned and grinned at Freddy. "Hello, you bum. Watch your language." I stuck out my hand and he grabbed it and pumped it up and down while I said I'd just got into town, and how's it going?

He shook his head. "The town's starting to roar. They been keeping me busy." Then he frowned. "Shell, I couldn't get a place for you. The whole Strip's jammed."

"It's O.K. Uh, learn anything else?"

"That Carter guy? Nothing. Blank. I guess I didn't do you much good, huh?"

I winced again, but this time because I wasn't anxious to have the name Carter bandied around too freely till I knew for sure what had happened to him. But I said, "Hell, it's good just to see you. You can make us even. Introduce me."

"Huh?" He tried to look puzzled. With that happy face he didn't make it. I didn't add anything.

So he frowned and looked at me and then at the lovely and then back at me. "I'm damned if I will," he said, and he grinned all over his face.

I looked at the girl again. "You're Irish," I said. "Eight to five you're Irish."

She smiled, and that all by itself made me feel good. She said, "You win. I'm Colleen Shawn. Pay me."

That little crackle in her voice made it sound almost as if she were catching a cold, but it wasn't at all unpleasant to my ears. It was fun to listen to her speak, but it didn't make you want to laugh at her; it was just attractive.

Colleen looked across the bar. "Freddy, do what the horrible man says. Introduce us."

He said frantically, "You don't know him. He's got a diseased mind. He's got a club brain. He's demented. He's a Communist. He's a super-spy. No! He's just an old spy failure. He sits in attics and eats cobwebs and thinks evil, evil—"

27

She was laughing with that same crackle in her laughter, but she waved her hand at him and said, "Oh, stop it. Come on, Freddy. Be sweet."

He said, "As you know, old pal, this is Mrs. Colleen Shawn. Mrs. Shawn, this ugly, broken-nosed neurotic is Shell Scott. He is a private detective and will probably lock you up."

I choked, because for a moment there I'd misunderstood him. "I'd like to," I told her. Then I asked, "Mrs.?"

"Not any more," she said, and damned if she didn't lift up her hand and dangle it before me like in days of old when people went around grabbing hands and kissing them. I'd be happy to kiss her hand, I'd be happy indeed, but I knew what I *wished* she'd dangled before me.

I took her hand in mine and said elaborately, "Mrs. Shawn," and feeling quite silly, I put her hand against my mouth and kissed the backs of her fingers.

She kept looking at me and said softly, "Mr. Satyr."

I twitched involuntarily, and she pressed her cool fingers tighter against my lips, and with her thumb and index finger she gently squeezed the corner of my mouth. And what happened to that wide-eyed innocent face was like eight ounces of adrenalin squirted into my blood stream. Her lips moved only slightly, and her eyes narrowed just a trifle, and she raised an eyebrow no more than a fraction of an inch, but I thought my vertebrae were going to go *clickety-clack* like thirty-three castanets and shiver into little pieces.

Then she took her hand away and said, "How do you do, Mr. Scott?"

"How does he do," groaned Freddy. Then, "All right, all right, I'm coming," and he walked down to get a very thirsty man a drink.

"Colleen," I said, "or is it Mrs. Shawn?"

"I'm not a Mrs. any more; I've had the six-week salvation here. And, anyway, it's Colleen."

"Tell me all about yourself," I said. "Everything."

She smiled slightly at that, and gave me a trace of the previous look, but she said, "You tell me something about you."

Usually men like to talk about themselves, and she undoubtedly knew that, because I was getting convinced that this was a wise woman indeed, but right now I was more interested in her. But so that we didn't go through one of those horrible you-tell-me-no-you-tell-me deals, I said, "Not much about me. I'm thirty, a bachelor, a private detective. Office in Los Angeles and an apartment in Hollywood. I think you're lovely and I'd like to monopolize you, only. . . " I stopped. I'd actually forgotten, for these last few minutes, what I was up here for.

She asked, "Only what?"

"Only—I think I may be pretty busy."

"Women—"

"That's not what I meant."

28

"—or private detecting?"

"Well, both, if *you're* going to be around town and if I don't get all wound up detecting." I almost added, "Or wounded up."

She smiled. "I'll be around through Helldorado, I guess. I'm just enjoying myself."

Somebody tapped me on the shoulder. It was Freddy. "What are you doing on this side of the bar?" I asked him. He picked up my left arm, pulled back my sleeve, and tapped my watch. "Where you been? It's after six. Come on up to the room and I'll give you the scoop on the housing situation."

"O.K." I turned to Colleen. "You staying at the hotel?"

"Uh-huh."

"I might give you a ring. O.K.?"

"I'm in One-o-seven. Or I'll be down here somewhere."

"Good enough. I'll find you." I turned and followed Freddy toward his room. On the way I stopped at the desk and Freddy waited while I checked on William Carter again. I was hoping to hell that he'd strolled in with mission accomplished, because this place was getting into my blood and Colleen was much on my mind, and I could think of any number of things I'd rather do during Helldorado Week than look for Isabel Ellis.

But it looked as though I might also wind up looking for William Carter, because the guy was still among the missing. At least Lorraine wasn't missing any more; not that that was good. The clerk on duty knew nothing at all about Mr. Carter except that he wasn't present or accounted for. I found out that the clerk who'd checked him in wouldn't be around again till tomorrow, then followed Freddy to his room.

Ordinarily Freddy lived in a rooming house farther downtown, but he was in Room 209 at the front of the hotel on the second floor for Helldorado Week. He was keeping it as a "base of operations," he said, and he didn't explain that. He didn't need to explain. When we got inside the room the first thing my eyes lit on was the bed, and I was surprised at how good it looked. Now that the noise and excitement weren't bubbling around me I could feel the fatigue sticky inside my body. All the running around I'd done this morning, and the long drive up here, added to the beating that had given aches and twinges of pain that were still with me, suddenly ganged up on me. I needed some rest. Even my brain was dulled with fatigue.

Freddy saw me looking at the bed. "Flop," he said. "I'll fix you something for your corpuscles."

I tossed my coat over a chair and flopped, and noticed that he had a paper sack under his arm. He pulled out a fifth of Old Taylor and a plastic sack full of those ice cubes with holes in their middles. He held up the bottle. "This is now your private stock, Shell. Welcome to the party. Now, what's your situation?"

29

I relaxed while he mixed the drinks in tall highball glasses he'd filched from the bar, and said, "Just what I told you on the phone, chum. Looking for a gal named Ellis who might be somewhere up here—or might be in Wisconsin, for all I know. This Carter came up here after her. You didn't get anything on him, huh?"

He grinned as he came over and handed me a drink. "Tell you the truth, I barely made it to work this morning, so I didn't have much time to nose. Been working all day. But I asked around the hotel people here. Nothing. Like you said—registered, but nobody's seen him since."

"Yeah. There's something damned screwy. I was warned in no uncertain terms to stay the hell away from here. And I think I got a welcome." I gave him the story of the robin's-egg-blue Chrysler and finished, "So I don't know whether I made an ass of myself or prevented a hole in my head."

He laughed. "You got holes in your head already, working at a time like this. Your car still at the airport?"

"Yeah."

"Good enough. I'll pick it up and bring it in while you relax."

I sat up on the bed. "The hell you will, Freddy! That car stays there till dark. I'll pick it up myself when I get a line on what's cooking. If I pick it up at all. The guys hate my guts up here, whoever they are, and they must know the car by now, even if they don't know where it is."

"O.K., O.K." He grinned. "What you want me to do?"

I was getting so tired and dopey lying on that soft bed with two pillows behind my head that I almost wanted him to do nothing but leave me in peace for an hour or two. Then a thought struck me.

"One thing, Freddy. This Angel of the phone. That wouldn't have been Colleen Shawn?"

He shook his head. "Nope. The Angel flew this morning. Just a tomato. Wish to hell it had been Colleen. You like that, huh?"

"I like that. Know anything about her?"

"Just that she shivers my timbers. I've only talked to her a couple of times at the bar. She's been around for a week or so. That's about all I know so far—but I'm gonna give you competition."

"Good enough. Say, Fred, I've got a call on a guy named Dante on my schedule. You know him?"

"Sure. Victor Dante. Runs the Inferno. Owns another club or two. Not in Vegas, though."

"I'm going to see him later tonight—if I can get off this bed. What can you tell me about him?"

Freddy scratched his black hair. "Gambler—a smart one. Understand he came up from L.A. One thing, Shell, you don't want any trouble with him.

He's got a lot of influence around here now. And that influence, they tell me, is not only political but police. Let's see, they opened the Inferno about three months ago. February, I think it was. He was around a while before that, but he's a real big man now he runs the Inferno. Moved right in. Tell you something else: He'll bet on anything, but from the dope I've picked up behind the bar, he's a sure-thing, boy. Doesn't like to lose. Don't even bet him the sun will come up in the east tomorrow, because he'd win if he had to put in a fix with some angels."

"Like that, huh?" I thought a minute. "The last thing I heard about this Carter guy was that he was going to call on Dante. That's the main reason I want to see him."

Freddy lit a cigarette and frowned at it for a while before saying anything else. Then he looked at me. "You watch yourself. It might interest you to know that the Inferno wasn't originally supposed to be called the Inferno. When they first started building the place it was going to be the Sundown Club. Most people know that, but not so many know a guy named Big Jim White was behind it then."

"Then? Why not now?"

He grinned. "That's a funny thing. Dante was interested in the place all along, but the story goes he didn't have enough cash to handle it. This Big Jim was on the inside—had the backing and money—but he got taken suddenly dead about a month before the club opened. Then there were some legal powwows, and now the place is Dante's Inferno."

"How do you mean, taken dead?"

"Accident. Apparently Big Jim was walking around on the highway out beyond the Flamingo and a car hit him. The sheriff wondered what the guy was doing there—not a damn thing out there—and he asked a lot of people, including Dante, about it. Wound up an accident, though."

"Interesting," I said. "Sounds like a convenient accident. For Dante."

I finished my drink. "I suppose I'd better get with it. Don't feel a hell of a lot like it." I put the glass on the floor and let my arm dangle over the side of the bed. It would have taken too much energy to pull it back up.

Freddy scowled. "You should get with some sleep. You look beat. How you gonna sleuth if you're dead?"

He didn't mean a corpse, just beat, but he'd made two points without trying. I was so tired I wasn't sharp, and if I were literally dead. . .

"Maybe you're right," I said. "O.K. if I pop off here for a couple?"

"Make it three," he said. "I'll call you around nine or so."

"Good deal, Freddy. Thanks. Maybe we'll get a chance to hang one on." I was almost asleep before I finished talking.

The sirens woke me up. And from there on in it was hell in Helldorado.

6

I WOKE UP slowly, the way I always do, and I heard the siren scream without even wondering, at first, what had awakened me. Even when I realized what was making the racket I associated it with L.A. for a second or two, wondering from force of habit where the boys were going. Then I remembered where I was as the sound of the siren grew from its faint beginning and shrilled inside my head when it passed the Desert Inn, going south on U.S. 91 out of town.

I shook my head and blinked, remembering the stuff I had to do. Had to see Victor Dante. And I wanted into Carter's room, too, to check his stuff, see if there was anything in it that would help me. It might be best to ask Carter about that first, though, if I ever got the chance. And I had to start showing that picture around. Maybe Freddy could help me there. He met a hell of a lot of people across the bar, though most of them were just blanks, customers, guys rapping with silver dollars.

I looked at my watch. Eight-thirty. Might as well get going. The better than two hours' sleep had done me a lot of good. I was a little stiffer, but otherwise I felt better. I started to get up and noticed that Freddy had tossed a blanket over me, and my cordovans were side by side on the floor. I grinned and got into the shoes, then splashed cold water on my face and began to feel human.

Another siren was wailing, getting closer, and I began wondering what was causing all the commotion. I walked to the front of the room and stuck my head out the window as cars started pulling over to the side of the road to let a black radio car race by with its red spotlight blinking. I knew the city limits were the other side of Bingo's on the downtown side of the Strip, and that the Las Vegas police department has jurisdiction over only the four square miles of downtown Las Vegas. And we were out in county territory here, so those would be county cars: men from the sheriff's department I watched the bouncing taillight of the car as it went up toward the Flamingo and swung left at the curve and out of sight. They were sure in a hurry, but there wasn't anything beyond the Flamingo except desert and McCarran Field. That was right, the airport was out there.

I got a little tickling sensation along my back. Maybe it wouldn't hurt to go out there and take a look. I made sure I had my .38, put on my coat, and went out and down the stairs to the edge of the lobby. I stood there for a moment remembering that I didn't have my Cad handy and I couldn't just stroll out to the airport. Then I remembered Colleen had said she was in Room 107. That was just off the lobby, around to my left here on the main floor, so I swung around, walked to her door, and knocked.

She opened the door and smiled when she saw me.

God, she was beautiful. I stared at her till she said, "Hi. Didn't know you'd be here so soon. You look like you're walking in your sleep."

"Think I am. Hi."

"Come on in, Shell."

"I'd like to, but I come asking favors. Already. You mind?"

"Depends on the favor."

"You got a car?"

"Last year's Mercury. Want a ride?"

"I thought we might start getting better acquainted by following sirens. I'm curious. O.K.?"

"Sure. That'll be different, anyway. Let's go."

She was still dressed the same way she had been at the bar and she looked just as good or better, and I noticed that in addition to everything else she had the most beautiful legs in a long, long time. She got another point on the good side when all she had to do in order to leave was take three steps to the dresser, pick up her handbag, and come on out. She pulled the door shut and we started.

Before we got into the looby, I said, "Hey, I'm not quite awake, and I didn't think. There's, uh, some people who don't like me. Even a chance somebody might take pot shots at me. Maybe I shouldn't have asked you to come."

She blinked at me and stopped. "Are you serious?"

"Uh-huh."

She shook her head, then shrugged and started walking again. That was all. I followed her to the car, a dark green club coupé. She slid under the wheel and zoomed out of the curving drive with the tires screeching. She seemed to like getting things done in a hurry. I told her where the excitement seemed to be and she ripped out the highway getting there.

The trouble was at the airport, all right. I told Colleen to pull in and she slowed down as we came to within a few feet of the center of activity. There was some confusion, and about twenty people were milling around over at the right of the airport building. The red spotlight on the top of one of the sheriff's black patrol cars pulsed bright and dim, bright and dim. I could hear harsh, impersonal voices barking orders and asking questions, and just then another car drove up with the siren muttering in its lowest register.

Always when I first awaken I go around in a sort of sleepwalker's trance for a few minutes. But I was awake now and I knew I'd wanted to come out here because I'd thrown airport-Cadillac-sheriff-excitement all together in my mind and got a fluttery shiver along my spine. I reached into my coat pocket to make sure the car keys were there and I couldn't find them. I sat up straight and went through all my pockets, but there weren't any keys.

And then I saw my car as some men moved away from the side of it, and at first, it's funny, but all I thought about was that my old ugly Cadillac was no good to me any more because the whole front end was ripped up, the metal of the hood twisted and gaping with holes and the windshield cracked and broken. It looked just as if a half-dozen sticks of dynamite had blown all to hell under the hood, and I started to grind my teeth together as anger boiled inside me and started to rise, and then it died out of me, died all the way out of me.

Because I saw why the men at the side of the Cad had moved away; saw the limp body they were placing on the ground; even saw them starting to cover him up; and I got cold all over, felt the cold brush over all my skin, and I said, "Oh, my God. My God. Oh, my God, Freddy."

Colleen said, "What's the matter? Shell, what's wrong?" But I couldn't answer her because my vision blurred all of a sudden and I couldn't do anything except put my forehead down in my hand and hold it and squeeze it as if somehow that could help take away the chill and the sickness. For a moment I didn't know what to say or even what to do, and then I got out of the car and walked over to the men gathered around the body on the ground.

34

He was already covered, but I got down on one knee and pulled back the cloth over him and it was Freddy, as I'd known it would be, and his face looked almost the same, what was left of it, but the worst was high on his chest.

I covered him up quickly because I just wanted to be positive, didn't really want to look at him at all. Then a uniformed deputy grabbed my arm. "Who the hell you think you are, Mac? Get away from the body."

I squeezed my hands into fists, then stretched them open and turned away from him. He grabbed me again, his eyes squinting at me. "What you doing here, anyway?"

"Just. . . noticed the excitement. Somebody told me about it."

"You know the guy?"

"I knew him. From the Desert Inn." Then I added, and it was hard to say it, "He was a friend of mine, is all. Bartender at the hotel."

"We know who he is."

"How'd it happen?" I asked him.

He acted as if he weren't going to answer, then he looked at the front of the Cad. "You can see, can't you? It blew up."

"Not by itself, Officer."

He shrugged. I walked away, wondering if he'd stop me, but he didn't. As I turned around I saw a man watching me, a man with a familiar face that I'd seen once before when he'd been looking at me from the near side of a blue Chrysler. He was about fifteen feet away, partly in shadow, and there was another man with him that I didn't recognize. The one I did know, a short, husky guy with a big nose and a bald head, turned to the other man and said something I couldn't hear.

I turned away from them and started walking from the airport toward the street, far ahead of me. The highway was straight ahead and for about fifty yards there was some illumination, then there was darkness with the road out there invisible from here. I walked by the Mercury and Colleen looked out at me and said, "Shell, what is it? Tell me."

I said, "Beat it. Get out of here." Then I kept walking toward the darkness with the airport at my back and the two men at my back, and I thought they'd follow me because *I* was supposed to have been in the Cad, not Freddy, and I hoped to God they did follow me.

You know how something like that hits you? There's shock that numbs you for a while just as if you've been hurt physically. There are physical changes in your body, and maybe the backs of your knees feel like water and your skin gets cold and perspiration jumps out on your forehead. If it's bad enough you can get sick or faint or even have a heart attack. It had hit me hard and the shock had momentarily numbed me, but I was coming out of it

35

enough already so that there was time and room for the anger to well up in me again. It was cold and brittle anger, and I knew it would stay with me for a long time.

I took one quick look over my shoulder when I was about fifty feet from the building. The Mercury was still there, Colleen hadn't taken my advice, and halfway between it and me were two figures outlined against the brilliance behind them. I turned around again and walked slowly, but I pulled the .38 from under my coat and held it in front of me. The Special is a double-action revolver, so all I had to do was pull the trigger.

I walked slowly, as if I were going nowhere, just walking away from what was back there, and I heard the footsteps, finally, close now. They came up almost to me and then the tempo of the footsteps increased suddenly and if this was anything at all, this was it. I waited another fraction of a second and jumped to my left, spinning around at the same time, and the little bald-head-ed man grunted and nearly stumbled as he tried to twist around, and he almost fell against the barrel of my .38. He stopped suddenly, his right hand a little above the level of his head, and the taller man behind him bumped gently into him as he stopped, too.

There was little light, but there was enough so they could both see the gun, and I moved it slightly and said, "Move an inch and I'll kill you. Now hold it, just like that."

They froze. The little man's right hand had been slowly coming down, but he stopped moving and stood with his hand almost even with his fore-head, a little bit like a man saluting. Only he'd been getting ready to salute me with a sap that hung down from his fingers and extended two or three inches farther down than the level of his chin.

"Start in talking," I told him flatly. "Who set that up back there?" I moved around them as I spoke so that what light there was came from behind me and fell full on them. I could see them plainly enough, but I doubted that any-one back at the wrecked Cad could see much, if anything, this far away.

Neither of them said a word and I pulled the barrel of the .38 over and held it two feet from Baldy's head and pointed right at his nose. He said sud-denly, "Just walking. Walking back to town."

"You son of a bitch! Drop that thing. You always walk around with a sap?" He dropped it. I went on. "Both of you, stretch. Hands nine feet up. Stretch!"

They put their hands high over their heads and stretched. I looked from one to the other. "Start talking, and do it fast or I'll ruin you, so help me. Who worked the job on the car? Why are you bastards after me?"

They didn't say anything and for about ten seconds I waited for them, and every second I got hotter and sicker and the knots curled tighter inside my stomach. One or both of these guys were going to tell me what this was all about or wind up half dead, and remembering what Freddy had looked like under that blanket, I wasn't sure I'd stop at halfway measures.

They didn't speak. I lowered my gun down to the level of my hips.

"O.K.," I said. I took one step forward, slipped my finger outside the trigger guard, and slashed the gun up in a fast arc that began at my hips and ended against Baldy's chin with a shock that I felt in the tight muscles of my forearm. He let out one small gasp and started to sag, but I grabbed the front of his coat with my left hand and flipped the gun in my right hand over toward the other man. He was down off his toes, standing flat-footed, looking at me, but I said, "Up! Stretch, damnit," and he almost went clear off the ground. While he was still looking it me I let go of Baldy, and as he fell toward my feet I slashed the revolver down and across the top of his head. He crumpled up silently at my feet.

The tall guy blurted, "For crisake, you might of killed him."

"You think you'll talk to me now?" I let him hear the double click as I pulled the hammer all the way back. The metal was a little slippery and I had to press harder than usual on the checked surface of the hammer, but it clicked twice and he heard it, all right.

"Hold it, wait a minute. I don't know nothing. He got me. Him. Abel. Nils Abel. Oh, Jesus."

"Who's Nils Abel?"

"Right there. You hit him." His voice was shaking.

"Keep it going."

He kept it going. He talked a blue streak with his voice cracking once in a while, but he didn't say anything I wanted to hear. He was Joe Fine, a local handy man: handy with a gun or sap—or anything requiring little intelligence, apparently. Nils, the guy on the ground, had picked him up earlier, saying that they might go out to the airport. Nils hadn't said why, but by now Fine did know that somebody—he didn't know who—had wired the dynamite in the Cad. I thought he was telling me all he knew. About the only other thing I found out was that Nils Abel was a box man at Victor Dante's Inferno.

Then light splashed full upon us. Headlights. I risked a quick look, then swung back to Fine, wondering what the hell I did now. It could be Colleen, or somebody of the curious, or the law. At first the law seemed one hell of a good idea, but out of the back of my brain I remembered Freddy saying something about Dante's influence: "Political and police." I wasn't in my own back yard now and there was no Captain Samson on my side or anyone else I could be sure about. Right now there was just me.

I didn't have time to stop and add up all the pros and cons, think it out logically, because while we stood there full in the glare of the headlights— Joe Fine with his hands over his head and me holding a gun on him, and

Baldy crumpled on the ground—somebody back at the airport yelled loudly and a bright spotlight on one of the sheriff's cars swung over and outlined us even better than before.

The first car slid to a stop alongside me. It was Colleen, and I made up my mind. I called to her, "Wait there," then swung the big guy around, eased the hammer of the .38 down, and reversed the gun, then smashed the butt against his skull. I was climbing into the Mercury before he hit the ground, and I looked out the rear window as a patrol car behind a screen of people backed away from the building.

I looked at Colleen and her face was frightened. "Baby," I said, "you can either sit here and wait, or get me the hell out of here."

She'd already had the gears in low and she let out the clutch with a snap that threw my head back onto the cushions. Then she skidded around to the right and hit the road leading out to Highway 91.

I said, "That's a police car back there. If you don't stop, you're in trouble."

She didn't say anything. She bent over the wheel, staring straight ahead, and had the gears in high and the accelerator jammed to the floor boards, and I heard that sound which is like a power saw slowing when it cuts through too heavy timbers, as the siren behind us shivered high at its nerve-scraping peak and began whining down the scale.

7

OLLEEN raced to Highway 91, skidded to the right, and flew down the road, past the Flamingo and the Inferno and the Desert Inn, entering the traffic that was heavier now back on the main part of the Strip. We'd picked up a good head start on the sheriff's car, because the deputies had to wait for some of the people to get out of their way or else run over them, and then had paused momentarily by the two men who might have been dying for all they knew. But they'd come after us.

I asked Colleen, "The cops know your car?"

"No."

"From back there at the airport, then? Think they'd remember it?"

"I don't think so. There were other cars there. I doubt that they could have noticed the license number; all that was so fast."

The Thunderbird was up ahead on the right. I said, "Slow down. Pull into the Thunderbird and park on the left. Douse the lights."

She zoomed into the drive and parked as cars on the road began pulling over and stopping in obedience to the siren. All the clubs on the Strip have a lot of parking space, and there were probably two hundred cars or more around us. Even if the deputies had seen us turn in here, which was doubtful, it would be like looking for the proverbial needle. A few seconds after Colleen turned off the lights and killed the engine, the black car raced past on the road toward downtown Las Vegas.

We sat quietly for a while, then Colleen said, "What's it all about, Shell?"

She deserved some kind of explanation, but I kept it short and told her, "Honey, I'm on a case; I'm working. Somebody up here is anxious to kill me. It must have something to do with the case I'm on now, or it doesn't make sense. But that was my car back there at the airport. I left it there this afternoon, and Freddy must have gone out to pick it up for me, though I told him to stay the hell away from it. He just saw a chance to do me a little favor, and. . . That's the kind of guy he was."

She didn't say anything for a moment, then she said, "I thought from—what you said—that it must have been Freddy. When you told me to leave I just sat there a while. I didn't know what to think, then I decided to follow you. I thought maybe you were walking back. Then my lights shined on you." She paused a moment. "Shell, that man on the ground. Was he dead?"

"I don't know. He might have been."

"I saw you hit the other man. That was pretty horrible."

I turned and looked at her. "Maybe so, Colleen. But what they or their friends did back there was pretty horrible, too."

"Oh," she said, and was quiet.

No official cars came in after us. Nothing much happened except that we sat quietly for seconds or minutes. I looked back toward the Thunderbird Hotel, on my right. Above the entrance the great neon bird glowed garishly, with its round red eye blinking, and fifteen or twenty people moved around in front of the lobby entrance, some of them going inside and some coming out to head for other spots on the Strip. There were half a dozen Western costumes in sight, and one couple in evening clothes.

Colleen said softly, "Like to ride out a little way, Shell?"

"O.K."

She drove downtown and turned left off Fifth Street into East Fremont Street. Up ahead was what most people think of when Las Vegas is mentioned. It was a blaze of lights and color and neon: gambling halls jammed up against each other on both sides of Fremont from Second on up to Main, for two solid blocks. Overshadowing all the rest was the big sign above the Golden Nugget on the left, and beyond that the huge mechanical cowboy pointed the way to the Pioneer Club with his animated hand and thumb. And the Las Vegas Club, the Monte Carlo, the Frontier Club, and all the rest. Colleen drove through slowly because the place was full of men and women and cowboys. A guy blew a bugle at us as we crossed First Street, and we had to wait a few seconds for a man on a horse to get out of our way at Main, where Colleen turned right and then swung back to head out of town. Then she drove like the wind all the way to Hoover Dam.

We got out and looked at the dam, and looked down at the water and the reflection of the moonlight. Colleen didn't bother me with questions or idle chatter; she slipped her hand in mine and we spent fifteen or twenty minutes out there before we started back. It was a bright moonlight night and the stars were clear; it was peaceful and beautiful. Neither of us mentioned Freddy again.

On the way back in I made up my mind about what I was going to do, and when we were back on the Strip I asked Colleen to let me off at the Inferno. She cut into the curving drive that all the Strip clubs have and stopped in front of the entrance.

She asked me, "Do I come in, too?"

"Not this trip. Maybe another night."

"I didn't think so. Shell, see me tomorrow?"

I got out of the car. "I'll do my best. I'm not sure just where I'll be. Maybe lunch or dinner—if I'm not chasing around somewhere."

"Swell. 'By, then."

She drove on out and down the Strip. I watched her go. I'd met her only a few hours before, and I'd never kissed her, hardly touched her except to hold her hand, but I could tell: This Colleen was getting under my skin, getting to me. Even after all that had happened this afternoon and tonight, sitting beside her in the car driving back from Lake Mead I couldn't keep her purely physical attraction, and her beauty, from crowding up in my mind.

I watched her go, then I turned around and took my first really good look at Dante's Inferno.

The Inferno was the newest and most fabulous of all the fabulous luxury hotels and casinos in what the home folks themselves refer to as Fabulous Las Vegas. The word when applied to the Inferno was no Hollywood superlative; it was an apt description. It was between the Desert Inn and the Flamingo on the desert end of the Strip, and the building was huge, surrounded by twenty acres of landscaped grounds and parking space, and fronted with ten thousand square feet of velvety green lawn.

Equally distant from the two sides of the lawn and out close to the street, a statue of Satan stood, forty feet high and bathed in a wash of crimson from spotlights at its base. The arms were bent at the elbows and raised out toward the street, the right arm higher than the head, the left at waist level, all ten fingers rigidly extended. The figure itself was slightly crouched, the evil head bent forward as if peering into the cars that passed all day and all night in front of it.

The front of the club was an intricate network of neon tubing, most of it glowing redly, and so fashioned that as the current was directed from one set

41

of tubing to another, the entire face of the building seemed to be covered with leaping flames that occasionally shot higher than the roof.

The entrance was rectangular, but above and around it was painted, on the face of the building and under the neon flames, the same face as that of the Satan peering down at the highway: a monstrous face with the gaping door for its mouth. And through the mouth a steady stream of chattering and laughing people walked, some coming out but more going in. The Inferno was getting a big play.

The facade was impressive, but it was like the frosting on a cake: there was more, and better, inside. I went in. This was another multimillion-dollar hotel, little different from the others except for the trimmings. And except for the casino: the gambling room called the Devil's Room. The main lobby was jammed with people milling around, and I headed through the crowd for the entrance, just off the main lobby, into the casino. The Devil's Room was larger by far than the lobby, and it contained, in addition to what looked like close to a thousand people, a hundred or so slot machines, roulette and crap tables, and a long bar parallel to the left wall. I made my way to the bar and ordered a bourbon and water, not only because I needed it, but because I wanted to look the place over and get the lay of the land before I tackled Dante in his den.

The really impressive thing about the casino was the walls themselves. The ceiling was black, and all four walls from ceiling to floor were covered with scenes that looked, quite literally, like hell. Or at least what one would imagine hell to be like. There were hundreds of naked figures: in chains, being consumed by fire, being whipped or beaten or stretched on racks. It seemed that all the tortures of all time were being employed on the straining figures, but on no face was there any expression of pain, or any expression at all. These were blank, set faces with dull, staring eyes, and all the faces were exactly the same. These were the eternally damned and the eternally dying who could never die, existing forever till all senses were dead and living itself was death. It made me wonder, idly, what heaven would be like.

I drained my glass, managed to get the bartender, and asked him where Victor Dante's office was. He pointed toward the back of the casino and said there was a door in the corner, a hallway beyond the door, and Dante's office was across the hall, on the right.

I walked through the crowd, went across the hall, and knocked on the door. A voice inside said, "Come in."

I stepped inside the door and stopped. Victor Dante sat behind a large black desk and he looked up at me and his face dropped fifty degrees, and finally he said, "You son of a bitch."

It was the same guy, all right.

8

I STOOD completely still for a second after I stepped inside the door, and the incongruous thought struck me that for a relative stranger in Las Vegas I was sure running into a lot of people I knew. First Lorraine, and now the frozen-faced, foul-mouthed character who'd been in her dressing room last night. I knew that when I had time to figure out what this meant it should help clear a few things up for me, but right now I just didn't have the time.

We both recovered about the same moment and we both came up with the same first idea, but I was faster than he was in the first place, and his gun was in the drawer of his desk. I snapped my right hand up and flipped out my .38 and he stopped moving with the drawer halfway open. This was Sure Thing Dante, and the only sure thing if he jerked out a gun was that he'd be dead, and he knew it. But he looked right back at the revolver pointing at him and his little, far-apart eyes were just as cold and dark and empty as the open muzzle of my gun.

I kicked the door shut behind me and glanced around the room to make sure we were alone. I said, "Just for calling me a son of a bitch, you son of a bitch, I'm going to bust your damned head. Imagine what I'm going to do to you for the rest of it."

This was the first time I'd heard him use ordinary words, and he said, quietly now, "You're a stupid man, Mr. Scott."

I was tired of this guy. He piled insult on insult. But I wanted to ask him so many questions I didn't know which of them came first. I picked one at random. "Tell me about Isabel Ellis, Dante."

He didn't say a word.

"I've got ways, Dante. I can open that foul mouth of yours. Maybe you heard about the two goons at the airport." I stopped. "You bastard, *that* was some of your work. And that's just one more thing to club you for."

He just sat there behind his black desk as if he were waiting for something, and then I realized what it was. I'd had my gun on him all the time, and he hadn't gone into that drawer, but I couldn't see his knees or his feet or the buzzer that was probably under the desk, and I knew damned well he was waiting for somebody to bust in.

I stepped toward him and I snapped at him, "Up! Get up! Back away from that desk and get on your feet." He was slow about it, but he moved. I walked over within a yard of him, the gun close to my side. "Get over to the door," I said. He took a couple of steps towards the door I'd come in by, then he stopped. "Damn it, move," I told him.

He was too slow about it, and I owed this guy plenty anyway, so I kept the gun in my right hand, pointed at him, straightened the fingers of my left hand, and with my thumb up and hand rigid I swung my arm around and chopped him under the left ear. It spun him around and he staggered and dropped to his hands and one knee. He stayed like that for a moment, moving his head slowly, and I put my foot against his bottom and shoved him as hard as I could.

His arm buckled and he shot forward, his face skidding for three inches on the carpet. "Now get the hell over there," I said, and the door opened.

He came in without any singsong patter, and it was my other acquaintance from the Pelican party last night, but the thing that surprised me was that he came in without a gun. Apparently that buzzer didn't mean trouble, but simply "You're wanted by the boss."

He didn't come all the way in, just one step, and he stopped so fast that about half the mass of dry hair on his head flopped forward over one eye, but he saw enough out of the other eye to scare hell out of him.

That eye rolled down at Dante on the floor, then rolled up at me, and I thought it was going to roll clear back into his head. But it stopped at me and I yelled at him, "Get in here. And don't try a thing."

My gun was pointed right at him, but he was still only about a foot inside the door, with his right hand on the knob, and he leaped backward, swinging the door shut, and was gone as neatly as if he practiced it every day.

Dante slowly got up off the floor. He put his left hand up to his neck and looked at me. Finally there was something in his eyes: There was hate there, for me, but there was pain, too, and he was breathing so hard the air hissed in and out of his pinched nostrils.

He looked at me but he didn't say anything, so I did. "You going to answer my question now, Dante? About Isabel? And one about William Carter? And Freddy Powell?" I knew he wouldn't, and I knew I had to get the hell away from here, but I had to try.

He barely opened his mouth. "You won't get out, Scott. You won't get ten feet away from the Inferno. Not alive."

He was probably right. I knew as well as he did where our friend had gone. For help. And help was what they had plenty of here. But I was going to get one step closer to being even with Dante before whatever was going to happen finally happened.

I know a lot of Judo from the Marines, and I know how easy it is to put a man out or kill him with just one hand or even the fingers of one hand. But there is absolutely no satisfaction quite like slamming a hard fist into the face of a man who has beaten you up and tried to kill you.

So I transferred the .38 to my left hand, balled up my right into a large horny fist, and stepped closer to Dante. He suddenly understood what I was going to do. He got it, all right, but he got it too late, and he'd barely started to move when I launched my fist up at him, my arm straightening with the muscles corded in my forearm, and my shoulder behind it and my body pivoting and slamming ahead behind my whole arm. I landed right in the middle of his mouth and gave my fist a little twist as it landed, and it made a hell of a loud noise. Then it was quiet for the length of time it took him to hit the carpet. He'd be out for quite a while, and he was never going to be very happy with his mouth again.

There was no way out of here except the way I'd come in, so I stepped over Victor Dante, went to the door, and opened it. There was nobody in the hallway yet, so I put the short-barreled .38 in my coat pocket and kept my right hand on it and walked back into the Devil's Room.

One thing about it, there must have been close to a thousand people here in the casino. This was the first night of Helldorado, and the citizens were getting off to a roaring start. There'd been a big parade during the day, bands playing, a rodeo, the feeling of a party when you're dressed up in costume. There'd been drinking, too, of course, because the bars in Las Vegas stay open twenty-four hours a day, and there was a sort of drunken excitement in the air.

I was glad of the crowd, because I didn't think even Dante would turn anybody loose with a gun to pop away at me in his own club—or in any

45

other crowd, for that matter. I didn't think he would, but it was small comfort because I couldn't be sure. And, anyway, even if I were relatively safe in here, I couldn't stay here forever, and outside I was gone. I *had* to stay with this crowd. I looked at my watch. After midnight. It wouldn't be dawn for five or six hours, and even though daylight might help me once I was outside, I knew for sure that I couldn't last in here that many hours. But walking out now would be suicide. The room of a horned devil was an appropriate place for me to be now, because I was sure between the horns of a dilemma.

I walked ahead through the crowd, wondering how a man might be killed in a bunch of people like this. There was always a chance for a knife in the ribs; or maybe some boy would know enough to twist my hand behind my back, yank and press on my thumb and little finger, and simply lead me helpless out of the place and into that long blackness. I didn't know what faces to watch for, but I had to keep moving. I was well into the crowd now and I'd been glancing at the door behind me, so I saw old Bushy Hair, the boy with the frightened eye, come through with two friends. Friends of his. At least I got a look at them as they split up, one going left, one right, one into the crowd after me. I wasn't hard to spot because my six foot two stuck the white hair on my stupid head up over most of the crowd. It had taken these boys a little while to get this close, but I figured it was undoubtedly because they'd taken time to set up men outside—and probably send more through the front.

I kept moving, and I could hear the buzz of conversation, and the dealers at the crap tables intoning, "Here goes; comin' out, we're comin' out. Ten. Ten's a winner." And at another table a dealer with a more poetic streak: "I have a new roller, a new bowler, are you set with a bet?" All very happy and carefree.

I moved through the crowd and looked at every face I could, and that's how I happened to see her. Just inside the entrance leading from here into the main lobby was one of the big posters that are displayed in all the hotels listing the acts in the current floor show. She was standing with her profile toward me, looking at the big poster about fifteen feet from her. But I knew what she was looking at, because she probably wasn't used to it yet, and right at the top it said, "LORRAINE," in big black screaming letters. Not "Sweet Lorraine," but it was the same terrific profile all the way down.

The long black hair wasn't loose as it had been when she'd done her fire dance, but was coiled in a bun at the back of her head à la Faye Emerson, and I was close enough to see the little button nose, and the way her full lower lip protruded a little farther than the upper one as she studied her name. The same other things protruded, too, just as they had at the Pelican.

I walked up beside her and when she turned toward me I said right in her cute little face, "You bitch. You damned murderous bitch."

46

Her blue eyes suddenly went wide and her mouth dropped open. "Whaat?" she gasped. "What? What do you mean?"

I was pretty close to that lobby entrance, and I had an idea that somebody would be there watching for me. There was. A slim, six-foot guy with a college-boy face spotted me and shoved away from the wall. He was a new one, but he was one. He walked toward me and stopped about five feet away.

I looked at him and asked him in a conversational tone, "Did they tell you what to do when you got to me?"

He blinked. He didn't know what to do. I'm damn sure I wouldn't have known what to do either. I still had my right hand in my coat pocket, and I shoved it easily toward him about two inches, coat and all. His eyes flicked downward, then back up at my face. He looked around at the crowd, licked his lips once, and went back to the doorway.

Lorraine said, "What in the world was that? And what did you mean?"

There was a little anger on her face now, but she looked puzzled more than anything else. I jerked my head at the collegiate type and said, "That's more thanks to you, too, probably. Maybe you don't know it, *Sweet Lorraine*, but I've got a good idea you killed a nice kid named Freddy Powell just as surely as if you'd shot him."

"What? You must be crazy!"

"Yeah? Tell me you didn't pass on to Victor Dante the information that I drove the airport limousine into town."

"Well, what. . . I don't understand."

"If you did, baby, let it be on your conscience. Because as soon as Dante knew that, he could figure I must have left my own car at the airport. That was all he needed to know. And he had somebody go look at registration slips and stick a very damned explosive bomb in the car so he could kill me when I picked the buggy up. Only a guy named Freddy picked it up for me and got blown all to hell."

She stared at me blankly for several seconds. Then she said, "I don't believe you."

"You don't believe the story? Or you don't believe they want to kill me? Which is it?"

She didn't say anything.

I asked her, "You think that last guy wanted to shake my hand?" She looked down toward my right hand, still in my pocket, and her eyes got wider. She'd seen that part, too. I said, "And there's probably nineteen more like him keeping me penned up in here. Even if Dante didn't want to kill me before, he will when he looks at his face. So, baby, you better make up your mind what side you're on. I don't know what the hell your angle is, but you're in *something* screwy, and right now you're turning my

47

stomach. You want to answer some questions about Isabel Ellis or William Carter?"

She looked at me out of those wise-looking eyes and pressed together those lips I'd thought were willing, and then she said, "I don't know what you're talking about."

I turned around and walked away from her into the crowd. No matter what she told me, it wouldn't do me any good until and unless I could get out of here—and I was worried. I couldn't afford any more foolish plays like busting in on Dante with my gun still in its holster. Even though I hadn't known till now that Dante and Frozen Puss were one and the same, I'd known Dante might very well not feel friendly toward me. Freddy's death had thrown me off balance a bit, and I couldn't afford anything now that shoved me off an even keel. No matter how callous it seemed, I had to say the hell with Freddy and everybody else, and concentrate instead on the health and welfare of Shell Scott.

I caught Bushy Hair's eyes on me, both of them, and he was watching me from about ten feet away, but he didn't rush at me swinging or even step toward me. Apparently they were content for the moment to keep me in sight, maybe work on me till I made a break for outside. And maybe they were waiting for the crowd to thin out, as it always does before dawn. I had a hunch that their knowing I had a gun in my hand helped them keep a reasonable distance, too. I circulated some more. I hadn't seen Dante again, but if he showed up things might get rougher. I was glad I'd clobbered him good.

Then Lorraine was alongside me again; she'd come up to me this time. She said, "I've forgotten your name."

That was sure going to break me up. That was the last straw. I said, "I'm Shell Scott, remember? And pretty soon I'm the late Shell Scott. Get the hell away from me."

"Please," she said. "Did you mean all that?"

"No. I was kidding. I was making a joke. You can die laughing at my funeral."

I started to walk away, but she grabbed my arm. My right arm. I jerked around and shook her hand off. "Keep your hands off my arm, damn it. Keep them off *me*."

Either she was putting on a good act, or else she was suddenly convinced, by the way I looked and acted, that I hadn't been kidding a bit. Because that cute face softened for a moment and the impudent eyes went wide, and she bit on her swollen lower lip. "Oh, I'm sorry, I'm sorry," she said, and it sounded almost as if she meant it. I didn't believe her worth a damn right now; I wasn't believing anybody for a while. But if there was one chance in a hundred she meant it, there was no point in passing it up.

So I said, "O.K., you're sorry, and I'm sorry, so forget it."

48

"Can I help? Can I help you?"

"Sure. Once I leave this crowd and get outside I'm dead. A whole mess of Dante's hired hands are wandering around in here glaring at me and I don't know what half of them look like and they must all know me by now. All you have to do is tell me how in hell I get out of here."

She said, "Oh," again, and her face pinched up a little, and she said, "You won't get out; you won't get out," as if it actually made a difference to her.

I said, "That's exactly—" and I busted it off for five wonderful seconds, then I said, "Well, hell, yes, I will, sweet patootie. Don't get lost." Because I'd just had me an idea.

It was the last of about fifty lousy ideas, and I almost threw it away with the rest. But I grabbed it and looked it over during those five wonderful seconds, and when they were up I knew what I was going to do. It might not work, but it was better than not even trying; and it had a good chance simply and solely because I was right where I was: Las Vegas during Helldorado, and smack in the middle of a passel of keyed-up, having-fun people.

It was an idea rooted in the very temper and atmosphere of Las Vegas itself. Downtown, the clubs are shoved right up against each other and sound and laughter bubble out the doors and into the street. Even the drugstores and barbershops have slot machines in them, and usually someone is sticking in nickels or dollars, jerking the lever and listening hopefully to the whir of the dials as he watches for the ultimate: the three beautiful bell fruits that spell jackpot. It's a something-for-nothing hopefulness, and prosperity is just around every corner. Not only downtown, but especially here on the Strip, where there's more beauty and money and glamour. All around me now there was the rattle and whir of the slots, the click of the ivory ball settling into the random niche on the roulette wheel, the voices of the dealers: "Coming out now, place your bets; nine's the point, nine."

And there was the smell of excitement in the air: the smell of money, of women, of whisky; the smell of a crowd with gambling fever, and lust in its nostrils. It was all around us; you could get drowned in it, swept up and lost in it. And this wasn't just everyday Las Vegas; it was Helldorado. Anything could happen.

So I started in. Shouts and laughter crackled in the smoky air as I walked through the crowd a little, listening to the people, looking at them. And the atmosphere was just right: It was wild, a little drunken, and charged with a what-the-hell-abandon that got in the bones and sizzled. Damned if I didn't think it would work.

I said to Lorraine. "Stick around. Maybe you can give me a hand—if you weren't kidding."

She followed along as I walked. There was big money on the tables tonight: stacks of blue and white and brown and gold and spotted chips.

49

Most of the people were having fun, but a couple of times at the crap tables I saw faces that were gone, blank, washed-out, and empty. Somebody who'd finished having fun when the fever hit him and he couldn't stop, couldn't let go, and it got brutal and the man part of him died and withered up inside him and he shoved it out there into Mammon's gaping mouth till there wasn't any more. That's part of Vegas, too, and those faces looked like the faces on the walls.

But most of it was just for kicks. A man's hand lingering on a woman's warm thigh, or brushing her breast; too-shrill laughter and honest laughter; and a kind of pleasant tension over all of it. And a number of women by themselves, as there always are at a time and place like this—and maybe there's a mink coat in the morning.

I was ready, and the crowd was ripe for plucking. Come on, Scott, be a magician or a dead man, but get with it. I picked my spot and went to the bar.

I got out my wallet, well stocked of necessity for a trip to Vegas, and pulled out a hundred-dollar bill, a ten, and a single. I caught the bartender's eye, grinned, crumpled up the ten, and threw it at him. He fumbled it, picked it up, and came over.

He looked at the bill. "What's this for?"

"For nothin'. 'S yours." I raised my voice a little. "Hell, man, I just picked up forty grand at El Rancho Vegas. Here." I shoved the single across the bar. "Gimme a water ball."

He grinned. He liked to see people happy. When they gave him ten dollars. He started fixing the drink.

And that "forty grand," though it didn't cause any sensation, hung in the air for a little while and fluttered. I was standing at the bar, at the spot I'd chosen, between two stools occupied by two blondes. The one on my right was slim and healthy-looking, wearing a red-and-brown cowgirl outfit; the one on my left was short and shapely, wearing a black velvet dinner dress, strapless.

The left one didn't even look at me; she reached slowly up to the top of her dress, already pleasantly precarious, and pulled it down an extra half inch. The one on my right said, "What's a grand?"

I said, "Thousand dollars. Money. Thousand. Drink?"

She had bloodshot brown eyes and too much make-up, but she also had a willing disposition. She said, "Love one."

I looked at the gal on my left, and she was a doll. I glanced at the bodice of her dress, doing its bit for the cause it had very nearly lost, and she raised two little fingers to her lips, and she coughed. She coughed and she coughed. She went, "*Choo, choo, choo,*" and then she said, "Whoops! Oh, my goodness."

She didn't have any cold, maybe, but she sure had a nice cough. And she sure had plenty of goodness.

"Golly, pardon me," she said.

I told her it was all right, she could cough all over me if she felt like it. She was as cute and cuddly as a kitten: about twenty-one, maybe a year or two over, and she had a little doll's face and a ripe, red mouth. The blonde hair was down around her shoulders, and a thick strand of it fell forward over her right shoulder and gleamed against the pale white skin.

She asked me, "You been gambling?"

"Like mad. Shooting craps. I'm hot tonight, baby; made nine straight passes."

"You like to make passes?"

I grinned at her.

"Oh, mister," she said.

My drink had been in front of me for some time now. I said, "Three more," and wiggled my head from blonde to blonde. I shoved the hundred across the bar. "Give me my change in dollars, will you?"

"Silver?"

"Paper."

People along the bar on either side of the blondes were looking at me now. I drained my drink chug-a-lug like they say, and picked up the second one the bartender brought. The girls both beamed at me and thanked me and I asked the bartender, "What's the biggest glass you've got?"

"Well, a chimney glass is. About eighteen ounces."

"Fill it with bourbon and water for me."

He blinked, but he went away on his mission. The blonde with the hot cold said, "What's all the dollars for, honey?" Already I was honey.

"I'm the new Rockefeller. With inflation. Tonight I'm throwing money away." She didn't know whether to be alarmed at such a horrible thought or pleased that she might get hit with some of it.

The bartender came back with a huge glass shaped like an old-style oil-lamp chimney turned upside down. It was full of highball. He said, "If you drink all this, it'll kill you."

I thought that was funny. I paid him, picked up my one-dollar bills and the big highball, and stepped back from the bar. In unison the blondes spoke. The one on my right piped, "Don't go 'way," and the one on my left said, "You're not *leaving*?"

I said, "I'll be back. Stick around."

I turned and there was Lorraine still behind me. She asked me, "Did you flip?"

I pulled her away from the bar and spoke softly. "Nope. You still want to help?"

She nodded, frowning.

"O.K., Lorraine. You saw all that business just now?"

51

"Could I miss it?"

"All right, now scatter. Buzz around and latch onto blondes and brunettes and redheads, men and women and grandfathers, anybody and everybody. Tell them you've found a crazy man. Point me out. I've just won forty thousand dollars. I'm off my rocker, I'm a live one, I'm drunk."

"But—"

"Get with it."

She shook her head, but she turned around. I felt so full of hell that I just let my hand come up gently, and I patted her gently, and she stopped stock-still and looked over her right shoulder like in that pin-up picture of Betty Grable, and she gave me a slow, warm smile.

Goddamn! Maybe I was about to be murdered, but these last few minutes were wonderful.

I wandered around making noises like a winner for ten minutes, so Lorraine would have time for what I'd told her, and during the ten minutes I bought a cowboy hat from a drunk for five dollars.

Then I let go of the gun in my pocket, put on my hat, crumpled the bills a slight bit in my right hand and spread them, and gripped my monstrous highball in my left hand. I walked out into the center of the crowded casino, stopped, cleared my throat, and yelled at the top of my lungs, "Yippeeeeee! He-e-e-elllldorraaado-o-o-o-o!"

About nine hundred startled faces swung around to look at me. I took a sloppy pull at my silly highball, then yelled, "Yeeeeaaah, dogies! Yippee-ti-yo!" And I hauled off like Dizzy Dean and threw a whole fistful of pretty green bills way up into the air, and they separated wonderfully and started fluttering down like green snow. Nine hundred faces turned up toward the ceiling, and about five hundred mouths dropped open, and they all looked very foolish. Then the heads, a dozen at a time, then two dozen, then just about every head in the place swung around to look at the crazy man. There was no doubt about it: I was the center of attraction.

Maybe I wouldn't be safe if I left the crowd, but if I could, by God, I was taking the damned crowd with me.

9

I DIDN'T get the whole nine hundred, but I got very close to thirty in no time at all. There were several couples, but my crowd was predominantly feminine, and I mean *feminine*.

I began wishing that this caper wasn't designed to keep me from getting killed, and that I really had won that forty thousand. But right away I realized the foolishness of that thought, because, though what I was thinking might have been slower, it, too, would have killed me.

After my apparent fit, a buzz of conversation had swelled up and few people drifted toward me. I heard snatches of conversation that I assumed were about me: "Yeah, that's the goof. . . " "Up at the bar. . . " "Hundred grand crapping?" "No, stupid, not Costello. . . " and so on. I kept up my act, pretending to be somewhat drunk, and I shouted come-one-come-all-everything's-on-me-and-yippee-ti-yo-I'm-a-ring-tailed-billionaire.

Evidently Lorraine had done her work, too, because it didn't take long for half a dozen gals and two couples to gather around me and start shooting questions at me. Then the two blondes from the bar joined us and the cute little doll face came up and grabbed my arm.

"Honey," she bubbled, "don't you *dare* throw any more money away. I couldn't stand it."

I gave a little wave of my hand and shrugged as if that money were for the janitor. Maybe it was. Most of it was still on the floor. My God! We were walking on it.

"'S nothing," I said. "I'm gonna take ever'body out and buy ever'body ever'thing."

A tiny, dark-haired cowgirl clapped her hands together and squealed, "Oooohh, this is fun!"

We were getting a bit of attention and more guys and gals, mostly gals, came up and the gathering grew like a downhill snowball. I saw Lorraine on the fringe of the swelling group and she shook her head and smiled when I winked at her. I was trying to act a little drunk, and I was a good actor. Those two fast highballs on top of what I'd had earlier were starting to feel mighty good inside me. I looked at my milkshake glass or whatever it was, and that was down about four inches too.

There was a mess of us milling around now and I repeated my extravagant claims and yelled, "Let's go," and yipped a couple of times. We just sort of surged toward the wide door. Some of the others yelled, "Yea!" and "Yo!" and some more exciting things as we moved, picking up drunks and curious and what-the-hell characters on the way.

We picked up speed and at least thirty of us, but probably a lot more, mushroomed out of the Devil's Room and poured through the lobby, laughing and whooping and scratching, and everybody, honest to Christ, having a wonderful time, even me. The damn thing was contagious, like the spread of sullenness and anger through a lynch mob, only with that kind of crowd psychology in reverse. This was fun for everybody and it caught you and got hold of you and you couldn't resist it. I felt so good that when I saw Bushy Hair standing almost helplessly in the middle of the doorway leading outside, I blew him a kiss. The crowd went through him or over him and he just disappeared. Poof, he was gone. I was a magician: Give me a wand and I'd light up the sky.

We billowed out of the Devil's mouth and spilled over the lawn and past the statue of Satan into the street. And the crowd grew. I was like a man standing on a busy street in New York or Los Angeles and pointing up and yelling, "Look! Look up there!" and all of a sudden finding hundreds of people around him stopping and looking. We were a magnet; people attracted by the noise and excitement joined us, came running, and the crowd mushroomed, doubled in five minutes, tripled in ten.

I had me a goddamned parade.

We were headed south up the middle of the street, headed toward the Flamingo, I guess, for it was the only big club south of the Inferno, but we were close to a hundred strong by now and hardly anyone knew or cared any longer what had started this; they just knew it was here and hopped on for the ride. It had started with me, but I was only the spark, and it had nothing to do with me any more, and all I wanted to do, myself, was just roll along, laughing and yelling with that fever growing in me as it grew in all the rest, and I felt as if I could walk forever, with somebody behind me hanging onto the tail of my coat.

I'd long ago lost track of the little doll from the left stool at the bar, but I didn't care, I didn't care at all, because I had all sizes and shapes and textures, and somewhere along in this I'd lost my drink and put my gun back in its holster and wrapped my arms around the two closest women, and one of them was the woman I'd really been looking for ever since we poured through the Devil's mouth: the luscious, lascivious Lorraine with the big, soft, beautiful everythings—and *she* was the one who'd been hanging onto my coattail so I wouldn't get away.

She said something, but I couldn't hear her because we were jammed into the middle of the crowd and there was a constant roar in my ears, but she pulled my arm down from her bare shoulders and put it around her, way around her, and I pressed my hand to her breast and held it there. Lorraine laughed, her white teeth gleaming and her tongue tracing a moist shine across her lower lip, then she said something else I couldn't hear.

The whole crowd staggered along like a drunken man—and most of us were drunk—weaving from one side of the street to the other, and we flowed around cars and I heard horns honking and blaring. Over at the left of the road I saw, sticking up into the air, the graceful red neon flamingo at the top of the club, and I knew we were going past the Flamingo, going clear the hell past it, and I remembered something about heading for there but I didn't care.

We roared past the Flamingo, the last club on the Strip, and nobody knew where the hell we were going because there was nothing ahead of us now except desert, but we kept on going. So help me Christ, we kept on going. I squeezed Lorraine and the other woman to me, though I didn't have the faintest idea what the other one looked like, and with Lorraine pressed close against me I was fast losing interest in anybody else, and suddenly we were at the edge of the crowd in the darkness and neither of us had to say anything.

I'm not sure whether Lorraine pulled me or whether I pulled her; I don't remember and I'll never remember, but we left the crowd and ran alone off into the desert, both of us laughing like crazy people, and I guess we were a little crazy, but finally we stopped and dropped to the ground, feverish and panting. I reached for Lorraine and pulled her to me, seeing her upturned face dim and pale in the faint light, and I could see the shine of her teeth gleaming whitely under her pulled-back lips.

It was suddenly quiet, with no sound from those we'd left far behind us. Our rapid breathing was loud in the quiet of the desert and the rush of my blood was a drum sound in my ears. I was dizzy, as much from the feel of Lorraine's body pressed against me as from anything else, and it seemed for a moment as if we were the only two people anywhere in this night and this darkness. Just the two of us pressed close, looking at each other with our faces inches apart, and then her face moved closer to mine and her lips softened and parted as I pulled her even tighter against me and pressed my mouth harshly to hers. Her lips were hungry and almost violent on mine as she wriggled on her back, pulling me close against her, heavy above her. Her tongue slid smoothly into my mouth, caressing my lips and tongue, and I wound my fingers into the top of her strapless gown and pulled it down to her waist, feeling the cloth slide between our bodies as it bared her heavy breasts. Then my hand was on the warm, taut swell of her breasts as she pressed her teeth into my throat and said tightly, "Damn you, damn you, Shell."

Her teeth pressed almost painfully into my throat as I traced my fingers over the smooth dim whiteness of her skin, caressed the soft satin texture of her thigh, and then her lips were on mine once more, moving against my mouth as she said again and again, "Now, Shell, now. . . "

The sky was flushing in the east when I walked through the Desert Inn lobby and stood at the foot of the stairs for a while, shaking my head. I sure was some detective. I'd left Lorraine a block from the Inferno because she said she wanted it that way and that there was no sense in my going back inside the club after what had happened there. She didn't know it, but I hadn't intended to go inside. Then there'd been a somewhat strained moment in the cold, horrible illumination of the beginning day during which we'd looked at each other and murmured nothing-phrases. I walked back to the Desert Inn and little happened except that I saw a lanky brunette walking down the road in her stocking feet with her high-heeled shoes in her hand. I didn't remember seeing her at the Inferno, but she must have recognized the ring-tailed billionaire, because she said something unintelligible and threw a shoe at me.

No guns had been aimed my way, but I was shot. Those stairs certainly looked steep. I was Shell Scott, the Cactus Kid: a worn-out, world-weary Atlas with fallen arches and noodles for muscles. But at least I was away from Victor Dante and I was half alive.

I contemplated getting down on my hands and knees and crawling inch by inch up those stairs, but it didn't seem like the thing to do. Not that I cared a damn about conforming to the approved and socially acceptable stair-climbing routine; I was just afraid if I once got down there I'd never get back up.

I went up to the second floor and down the hall and stopped. Suddenly I felt sick, and it had nothing to do with the liquor or anything else. I'd gone, without thinking, back up to Freddy's room, as if nothing had happened and he'd be glad to see me. But finally I went on in. There was no other place for me to stay, and the room was no good now to Freddy.

Some of his things were still scattered around the room. I went on into the bathroom and showered, then turned out the lights and went to bed. I didn't go to sleep right away, even as tired as I was. There were too many things on my mind, too many unexplained angles. I'd come up here to look for Isabel Ellis but it didn't look as though I'd accomplished a thing. I was on a treadmill, running and running and running, and not getting anywhere. From the moment I'd hit town until now, somebody had been after me, pushing me, rushing me, and that meant something all by itself. But I hadn't even had time to do the simple, beginning things, the groundwork. I hadn't even unpacked my bag, and the picture of Isabel was in there still. I wanted to show that around; I wanted to go to the police, check with them on both Isabel and William Carter; and I wanted to check the funeral homes, because the more I thought about it, the likelier it seemed to me that there was where I'd find them.

At least I knew a few things and could add them together for something. I knew now that Victor Dante was the man who'd been talking to Lorraine at the Pelican-just the night before she'd shown up in Las Vegas—and that is was he and his sidekick who had beaten hell out of me simply to convince me I should *not* talk to Lorraine, *not* look for Carter, and *not* come to Las Vegas.

And Dante was acting like other men I've run across in other cases: like a man covering up his tracks, or a trail. And it appeared, now that I was hounding him, that he wanted me covered up, too.

Thinking drowsily, with the thoughts threading lazily among other pictures and memories in my mind, as they will when you're resting on the soft edge of sleep, I thought: Wouldn't it be funny if Dante had, for some reason or other, murdered Isabel—who had suddenly disappeared and wasn't being heard from these days—and then a detective hired by Isabel's father had stumbled onto proof of the murder and been killed because he had stumbled? It didn't fully explain what Dante had been doing at the Pelican Club, but that *was* where Carter had apparently picked up the trail, and if that was the answer, or part of it, Dante would be almost sure to resent my snooping around.

My thoughts were sluggish and circling and elusive, but almost the last thing I considered was that I had busted in on Dante at the Pelican and, right after that, started asking questions about Carter and Isabel, and that now Dante knew I was aware of his identity since we'd met at his Inferno. I was thinking that it looked as though Dante would have no other choice but to kill me, when I fell asleep.

I wouldn't know it until later in the day, but they'd already found Carter's body.

10

I WOKE UP about two in the afternoon and lay in bed for five minutes, clearing the fog from my brain and remembering the thoughts that had been in my mind when I'd fallen asleep. After that I groaned out of bed and spent five minutes more in a hot shower, soaping my bruises. I was going to be sure I was awake before I started charging around this day.

I opened my bag, got out the shaving tools, and scraped the stubble off my chin, then got dressed in a tan tropic-weight suit, clean white shirt, and dark brown tie. I included the .38 as part of my outfit, then went down to the Cactus Room, just off the lobby, for breakfast.

The hotel was jumping like crazy and I remembered that this was still the four-day Helldorado, and this was only the second day. But by the time I'd forced myself to eat a good breakfast, because I might not get a chance to eat more than my nails for a while, I felt pretty good. The aftereffects of the L.A. working-over I'd received were still with me, but not as much as I'd expected. All that exercise last night must have loosened my muscles.

After two cups of black coffee I went to the desk, used up some more money, and slyly asked the clerk if there were a room available and if I could get a peek into Carter's room for a quick look around. I learned there wasn't any room empty yet, but all wasn't lost because I could look at Carter's stuff. It was a waste of time and money. All I learned was that Carter still hadn't shown up, and that he had a lot of clean white shirts he hadn't used. There was nothing in his room that helped.

I got the eight-by-ten photo of Isabel from my bag, called a taxi from the hotel, had another cup of black coffee while I waited, then climbed into the cab and went directly to Second Street between Carson and Bridger in downtown Vegas, and got out in front of the courthouse. I went up the steps and inside, then down to the sheriff's department on the main floor and identified myself to the man behind the counter. He squinted at me for five seconds, then sent me into an office on the other side of the counter to see one Arthur Hawkins. Hawkins was a big man sitting relaxed behind a pine desk, and he was a lieutenant. He hunched the coat of his dark gray single-breasted suit forward on his thick shoulders and glanced at me when I came in.

I said, "How do you do, Mr. Hawkins? I'm Shell Scott, an investigator from Los Angeles. I figured I'd better—"

He swung his head up, and I saw he was about forty, with wrinkles around dark eyes and deep creases at each side of his nose.

He said, "Where the hell have *you* been?"

"Huh?" Then I got it. "You mean the car?"

"I mean that miserable Cadillac. That yours?"

Naturally the deputies would have found the registration slip or what was left of it in the Cad, and would have checked on it. I said, "Yes, sir. That is, it was."

"Sit down. Right there. What do you know about that?" He clipped the words out fast, in little spurts like bullets. "We've been looking for you. Sarah!"

He had yelled out the door and halfway downtown. A girl flew in from the next room. She sat down in a chair in the corner, with an open steno's pad in her left hand. Hawkins nodded to her and she said, "Yes, sir."

"Hey!" I yelped. "Whoa, slow this up. You're all—"

"Siddown. Sid*down!*" The guy wasn't brutal or shoving me around; he was just nine yards of authority. He was overpowering. I stood still for a moment, just so he wouldn't think I overpowered easy, but I sat down.

Hawkins looked at me. "All right."

I deliberated a moment, wondering what the hell I should say, and he said rapidly, "Come on, come *on!*"

Well, damn him, damn him to hell. I stood up, and he could scream at me to sit down till he was hoarse. "All right, damnit," I said. I took out my wallet and tossed it on the desk. "There's my license; I'm a private detective from Los Angeles and you must already know that by now. You must also bloody well know I'm clean and I don't go around blowing up my own cars or spitting on sidewalks." I'd been getting nothing but lumps and shoving around up here, and now this razor-voiced lieutenant was slicing at me, and little red spots were getting ready to pop in front of my eyes. I leaned on the desk. "This is one lousy welcome to your lousy town. I'll tell you what the hell happened to that Cad of mine. I drive up here peaceably on legal business and a son named Victor Dante blows up my car, that's what happens. And I wouldn't be a damn bit surprised if he murdered a couple of other people up here—one Isabel Ellis and one William Carter—and murders me before he's through."

Boy, I sure put my foot in it that time.

He sort of shook when I said William Carter, and right then I knew Carter was dead. I stopped.

Hawkins looked over at the girl. The girl was getting it all down. She was getting every pearl that spilled from my big loud mouth.

Hawkins looked back at me. "This Carter, this William Carter. He's murdered, you say?"

"Well, I don't know. I just guessed."

"You guessed it. Well, you know what? That was a very good guess."

"He's dead, huh?"

Hawkins made it easy on the girl. He said not a word.

I started in saying words. I rattled them at him faster than he'd snapped them at me. I told him how I was hired, what had happened then. I just blocked it in sketchily, without any details such as my leaving the Inferno—and I sure as hell didn't tell him about my two-goon ruckus at the airport—but I let him know why I figured Dante was my boy.

We went round and round and the air got blue, but finally it cleared a little. Because apparently Hawkins didn't know I was the airport "fugitive" and also because I could account for all of my time in Los Angeles from May eighth till I'd left L.A., and sometime in there, as I learned from Hawkins, Carter had been murdered with three little .38-caliber slugs in his back. And, actually, all I'd said was that I thought William Carter was dead.

After half an hour I said, "And, Lieutenant, I walked in here pleasantly of my own free will for two reasons: to see if you had anything on Isabel Ellis, whose picture I've shown you, which you say you don't; and to see if you could tell me anything about Carter, which you have. And Carter was on this same job just before me, Hawkins. Grant me that my nerves might be a little on edge."

"You got up here last night?"

"I did."

"You didn't rush right down here for help."

"No, I didn't. Actually I was, well, on another phase of my investigation. And sometimes I'm not happy wandering around in the dark. I was supposed to be in that Cadillac, and whether you believe it or not, there's a good chance I'll wind up like Carter."

He sucked on his teeth and looked at me.

"One thing," I said. "Do me the courtesy of phoning Los Angeles. Captain Phil Samson, Central Detective Bureau, Homicide Division, in the City Hall."

He looked at the girl. "All right, Sarah." Sarah closed her notebook and went out. Hawkins leaned back in his chair and pulled the phone over to him. "I'll do that. Let me tell you something, Mr. Scott. I already have a pretty good report on you. And I, personally, would like very much to hang something on Victor Dante, believe me. But he is a man with much power and many friends, and there seems to be nothing. . . wrong with him. You give me something solid and I'll talk to Dante. I'm not going to look at him just because you have some wild ideas."

"Not that I mean to contradict you flatly," I said, "but they don't seem wild to me." I gave him a very slight grin. "It's just that he seems bound and determined to kill me. And, Hawkins, speaking of killing, isn't there something about Dante and a guy named Big Jim White?"

He frowned at me for a long time. "Nothing that holds water," he said finally. "I talked to Dante himself when he was questioned down here. Officially that was an accident. Where'd you pick that up?"

"Just heard somebody mention it. Does seem like something's screwy there, though, doesn't it?"

"Well," he said, "could be." He made the call to L.A. He spent five minutes on the line, without giving the phone to me, then hung up. I knew he'd talked to Samson, but he didn't pass on any of the conversation except to inform me that Sam had said to tell me he'd just sent me a telegram. That was something I wanted to see.

Hawkins told me about the telegram and added, "About Dante—or anyone else, Mr. Scott—you can't put a man in jail simply because one or two citizens get an idea into their heads that he should be there. Just as, for example, we're not holding you." He gave me a little speech then, beginning, "The laws are designed primarily to protect the innocent—" and I was ready to leave.

There was one last thing. The body of William Carter was in the Gruman Funeral Home, there being no morgue in Las Vegas, and Hawkins went over there with me. It was the same guy, all right. The same red hair and red mustache, and the jagged scar over the left eye. I looked at him stretched out in the funeral home, remembering that sweet voice back in L.A. trying to talk above the sound of the squalling baby, and I couldn't help wondering if I'd wind up like this: on a slab in a morgue or funeral parlor somewhere, with bullets in my back. Or maybe face down in the desert with blood and dirt on my mouth, as they'd found him.

61

Before I left I talked to Hawkins a little more. I assured him I'd take care of my wrecked Cadillac. He was a nice enough guy; he just didn't quite believe me.

He said again, "Give me something solid, Scott."

I said, "All right, Hawkins, maybe I haven't got anything good enough. But I'll tell you what I think now: Dante murdered Carter; he was responsible for killing Freddy Powell; he's after me; and I've got a fat hunch he killed one Isabel Ellis."

Hawkins sucked on his teeth.

I turned around and beat it. If they hauled me in on a stretcher, he was sure going to feel put out.

At the desk of the Desert Inn I picked up the telegram from Samson. This would be the info on Harvey Ellis I'd asked Sam for. And I was lucky another way at the desk; my money might have helped, but at least they had a room for me. It was 213, on the same floor as Freddy's room.

I explained to the clerk about my spending the night in Freddy's room and started to go on, but he broke in.

"Say, I'm sorry, sir, but if you have anything in the room you'll have to get it out pretty quick. They'll be cleaning it up soon. We have a reservation for four P.M."

How do you like that? Rented already. It was good sense and good business, but it griped me a little, anyway. I scribbled "Shell Scott" on the registration card, thinking I was the boy who'd decided to be callous, then got my stuff from Freddy's room, took it to my own room, and flopped on the bed.

Then I read the telegram. It said:

HARVEY ELLIS CONVICTED SECOND DEGREE BURGLARY AND SENTENCED ONE TO LIFE IN APRIL 1950 PAROLED QUENTIN JANUARY 1951 PAROLE ADDRESS 1644 FLOWER STREET LOS ANGELES IF NOT KILLED SEND CIGARS

I read the telegram again, then a third time, wondering what this meant, if anything. It was more than I'd bargained for, so I picked up the phone and called Samson.

When he came on I said, "Hi, Sam. This is Shell. Thanks for the assist with Hawkins a while ago."

"Get lost," he growled, and I knew by the sound of his voice that he was trying to keep the inevitable cigar out of the mouthpiece. He said, "I told him you escaped from the bughouse. Must have scared him."

"Yeah. Say, I got your wire. What's with Ellis? Can you fill me in some more? What was the caper? And I see he pulled the minimum, so it was his first fall, huh?"

"First time he got caught," Sam growled. "But that's not why he got out after only nine months."

"O.K. Give, Sam."

"The Burglary boys had an idea about four other big jobs with pretty much the same m. o. as the one Ellis got caught on. Somebody picked up a pile of cash and some negotiable paper. All in about six months before this Ellis caper, and they thought there was a chance he was the one pulled them."

"Well?"

"Still just an idea. Ellis said they were nuts, this was the first time he tried anything like that."

"Uh-huh. He'd hardly say anything else."

"Yeah. Burglary wasn't too convinced, either. That's part of the reason for the nine months, Shell. If he had the stuff stashed away somewhere, they thought he might head for it when he got out. It's probably a pipe dream. Ellis just settled down and got a job."

"Uh-huh. These four big ones, Sam. How big?"

"Plenty. All told, close to a quarter million."

"Jesus H. Christ," I said. "I'm in the wrong racket."

"You're not in jail, either. But you can see why the boys were willing to take the long chance it was Ellis. A quarter of a million bucks is quite a pile."

"Buy a lot of bourbon," I said. "How'd they get him?"

"You know the old Springer mansion off Figueroa?" I told him I did and he said, "That was the place. Daylight job again, nobody home, and no gun, so it was second degree. The old boy's supposed to keep heavy sugar in the house but Ellis didn't get any."

"Stop bragging for Burglary, Sam; you're a Homicide man. I know you're hot stuff."

He chuckled. "This time the hot stuff was very old stuff. Anonymous phone call to Burglary. Some babe spotted him busting in the back way and spent a nickel."

"Such efficiency," I said. "Such—hey! Sam, I just thought of something. You said a woman called."

"No!" he interrupted me. "Don't say it."

"But, Sam, Ellis' wife is a woman. Don't you—"

"Well whaddayaknow," he growled. "His wife is a woman. I know, I know," he went on, "she's nowhere around and that's who you're looking for—and it was even hinted by some of the boys that it could have been his wife. You and your feeble brain are gonna be the death of me. It could also have been any one of about two million people." He paused. "Well, that's it."

I laughed. "O.K., Sam. Good enough. I'll call you."

"Hey," he yelled. "What about my cigars?"

63

He'd get his Coronas, but just for hell I asked him, "What did you say?" and hung up. I wondered some more, then dug into my bag and got out the photostats and some of my scribbled notes and went over them. Isabel had used her maiden name, of course, and Isabel Mary Bing and Harvey Colin Ellis had applied for a marriage license in L.A. on January 14, 1939, and been married by Horace Mansfield, Minister of the Gospel, on January 18, 1939. Isabel had been only seventeen to Harvey's thirty-seven, which checked with the birth dates I'd noted: Harvey, February 2, 1901; Isabel, October 14, 1921. Both were natives of Los Angeles. Her mother, who was dead, was Mary Elizabeth Green before she'd married Isabel's father, Jonathan Harrison Bing. There was more stuff, name and address of witness, address of the minister, and signatures of both Isabel and Harvey.

Then I remembered something and picked up the telegram from Sam again. Isabel had sold her house on December 6; and J. Harrison Bing had told me he hadn't received any letters all this year, which would seem to put the last letters back in December. And I'd just learned from Sam that Harvey Ellis had been released on parole in January. It was something else to add to the little things that were accumulating.

I looked at the eight-by-ten of Isabel. In the picture she was smiling prettily, looking quite a lovely and mature woman with well-shaped lips and big eyes. Regular features, and dark hair worn in an upsweep. She'd have been a pleasant fixture at the Pelican—and that reminded me that I wanted to see Lorraine again. I'd seen quite a bit of her last night, true, but I hadn't learned any more from her—not about the case.

I put in a call to the Inferno, did *not* say who was calling, and asked if Lorraine—the floor-show Lorraine—was staying at the hotel. All I learned was that she had a room, wasn't in it, and couldn't be reached. I hung up thinking I could try again later.

So I tucked my eight-by-ten photo under my arm and went down to the lobby. I didn't have to wonder about Carter's disappearance any more; now I could concentrate better on Isabel. And I realized then that I'd been guilty of a cardinal fault in any kind of investigation: jumping to conclusions. I hadn't really been thinking about looking for Isabel, but for Isabel's body.

I stopped at the desk and showed the picture to the clerk and asked the right questions. This was as good a place to start as any.

He shook his head. "I'm sorry. I'm new here, sir. I don't know many of the people yet."

I thanked him and went to the bar. I ordered a drink and went through the picture routine before I realized this was a new guy too. He'd replaced Freddy. When a man dies he leaves only a very small vacuum where he was, and that fills up quickly.

I played with my drink and looked around. The casino was getting a good play. There were already half a dozen smartly groomed women around the near table.

I noticed one in particular, in tailored brown slacks, low-heeled shoes, and a black sweater. I noticed her because she was leaning with her left arm on the wide leaning rail, her right side toward me and her face turned toward the action on the green felt, and she stood out.

She was only an inch or so over five feet tall, but she was trim and firm and looked compact, with a little extra spilling out fore and aft. Maybe part of it was her position, and another part the angle from which I was looking at her, but that couldn't have accounted for more than 10 per cent of the beautiful picture I got. Standing like that, she reminded me of what Hogarth called the "Line of Beauty," which is a serpentine or S curve, and standing there at the table, she had it. It started high in front and looped out and then in at her waist, and then reversed itself and flowed down in an eye-straining curve and neatly tucked itself in. Honest to God, she must have had the most delightful bottom in all of Las Vegas.

I had work to do, and duty never called more faintly, but I pulled my eyes away from those curves and finished my drink. I got up and walked down the bar toward another bartender. I looked back over my shoulder once, though, and I couldn't help thinking of Hogarth again. That sure was a cute little S.

I climbed onto a stool and the bartender came up. I showed him the photo. "Ever see her around?" I asked him.

He glanced down at the portrait and shook his head. "Don't think so. Why?" Then he bent closer to the photo and picked it up. "Well," he said, "how about that?"

I sat up. That's what I wanted to know. "You know her?"

"Well, I'm not sure," he said. He squinted. "Does look a little like her, though, doesn't it?"

This guy was driving me nuts. "Like *who*? Whom? Who? Looks like what?"

He blinked at me. "Oh, I thought you knew. You were falling off your stool leering at her." He grinned as if that were the funniest remark of the day.

He must have noticed something peculiar happen to my face, but he beamed at me and kept chattering away. "She comes in most every day. Always drinks stingers and leaves me a buck. Not bad, huh? Wish I was Dante."

"What!"

He blinked some more. "What's the matter? Didn't you know she was Mrs. Dante?"

I didn't say anything for a full ten seconds. I couldn't. Then I said, "Bartender, give me a drink."

65

He shook his head, but started mixing a water-high for me. I swung my poor dazed head around for another look, and for one panicky moment I thought she'd gone, but then I saw her moving away from the dice table, turning away from me, walking to the far end of the bar. Even as rattled as I was, I couldn't help thinking that a walk like hers couldn't have been an accident: It had to have been planned, practiced, and perfected.

She slid up on the stool and ordered a drink, and the other bartender fixed her a stinger.

Mrs. Dante, Mrs. Dante, Mrs. Dante; it went ricocheting around in my skull. But the bartender had said, "Looks a *little* like her." There was no point in continuing to leap at conclusions. But if she were Mrs. Dante, maybe others of the Dante clan might be around. But how the hell. . . I stopped thinking about it for a moment and looked at every face I could see in the crowd. And, still at the dice table where I hadn't seen him before because I'd been looking at something much prettier than his stupid face, was Dante's right-hand man with the long dry hair swelling out over his temples, and the deep bronze skin, and the frightened eye. He hadn't seen me, apparently, and I didn't want him to see me. I asked the bartender, "Who's that mug?" and pointed him out.

"Guy from the Inferno. Lloyd something or other. Don't know just what he does down there."

"I know what he does. Thanks."

I took my drink and photo with me, walked along the bar, and sat down right next to Isabel Ellis or Mrs. Victor Dante or Julie-Belle Smutch or whoever the hell she was. She barely glanced at me, but I looked at her good.

I didn't know. Could be, though. The girl in the picture was a brunette with lots of hair, and this one had a feather cut that was blonde, almost platinum, but that could have been peroxide and scissors. And the girl at the bar was a few years older, apparently, than the one in the photo, but she was still a year or two either way from thirty as near as I could tell. The features seemed much the same; there was a difference, but it might have been accounted for by make-up. That trim figure looked as if she were careful about keeping it in shape: like a gal who played tennis, or took a lot of exercise, or visited masseurs regularly. But I didn't have a picture of her figure for comparison. Wish I had.

But just looking was telling me nothing, so I sat my drink on the bar, said, "Pardon me," and when she turned to me I handed her the photograph.

She had a pleasant look on her face, half-smiling as she took the photo, and I said bluntly, "Is that you?"

She looked at the picture in her hand, laid it slowly on top of the bar, and the pleasant look faded, washed right off her face, and she didn't make a sound. She just fainted dead away and slid off the stool to the floor.

11

S OMEBODY YELLED.

I grabbed the picture in one hand and bent over the woman. People crowded up around me and I didn't know what the hell was happening. All I could think of was that pretty face getting blank, and her toppling, and me watching her, too startled even to grab her as she fell.

I backed away as somebody picked her up and carried her over to one of the flat leather seats beyond the tables. She was starting to come around. And then I saw that the guy carrying her was goon-boy Lloyd. I didn't know if he'd noticed me in the excitement or not, but if he hadn't, he was likely to in a minute. I also realized that it hadn't been my job in the first place to barge up to the gal even if she *was* my client's daughter. When I'd been hired, Bing said if I found her and she was O.K. he didn't want her bothered; he merely wanted to be sure she was all right. But there was something I could do right now. I could call that guy and give him a piece of my mind before I got a hole in it.

I went across the lobby and up to my room without looking back. Inside, I grabbed the phone, fished in my pocket for the card Bing had given me, and gave the number he'd written on it to the operator.

67

He was in. After he said hello, I lit into him. "Listen, you old—" I busted it off and started over. "Listen, Mr. Bing, what the hell did you get me into up here?"

"What? Who is this?"

"This is Scott, Shell Scott, remember? Have you heard from your daughter?"

"Isabel? Why, no. What's the matter? You sound excited."

"Excited! You damn bet I'm excited. People keep trying to kill me, and I think I might have just seen your daughter."

He busted in right there. He practically swooned.

"You did? Then she's all right? Where was she, Mr. Scott? Is she all right? You didn't talk to her, did you?"

"Slow down a minute." I slowed down, myself, thinking. Then I said, "Actually, Mr. Bing, I'm not a damn bit sure of anything yet. You might say I'm confused. I may have seen Isabel and I may not. I simply don't know. Can you give me a better description of her? And how about this: Do you know of any reason why she might change her appearance? Dye her hair, things like that?"

He was silent for a few seconds, then he said, "Change her appearance? No, Mr. Scott. I don't understand. Is she—is she in trouble?"

"Frankly, you've got me. But listen to this, and listen good. If you know of any reason why she might be, you damned well better not hold out on me if you want me to stay on the case, and you know what I mean. I don't care if it makes you so uncomfortable or embarrassed you can't stand it. Now, why the hell didn't you tell me that Isabel's husband was an ex-con?"

There was another of his silences, then he said, "I'm sorry you found that out, Mr. Scott. I don't see how that could be important. The fact that my son-in-law is a criminal is hardly the type of thing I'd care to—"

I broke in on him again, trying to keep my voice level. "Mr. Bing, please listen carefully. Anything, believe me, anything at all might be important. If you'll let me decide what is and isn't, I might stay alive longer."

"I'm sorry, but there's nothing else you don't already know. Nothing. *Tell* me, is she up there? Is she all right?"

There we were again. I said, "I honestly don't know. Can you tell me any way of positively identifying her? You know, defects, scars, habits?"

He said hesitantly, "No-o. You have her picture."

"Yeah, I know. That's not good enough. I mean something else. Something positive."

"Well. . . I'm afraid the only scar she has wouldn't do you much good. When she was a little girl part of a tin can hit her—you know how children play with firecrackers, putting them under cans. Well, the can blew apart and cut about a four-inch gash on her cheek. But that's all I can think of."

68

"What's the scar look like?"

"Just a straight scar with a sort of sharp hook at the end, a bit like an arrowhead. But I'm sure that can't help you."

"That takes care of that, anyway. The gal I was thinking about didn't have any scar. Smooth complexion, for that matter."

"Ah, that's not exactly what I meant. The scar is on her. . . posterior."

I blinked. "You mean her fanny?"

"Well, yes, you might say that."

This time *I* was quiet for a while. There might be a scar on that superior posterior, but I didn't know what good that did me. Finally I said, "Nothing else, huh?"

"No. Just what is the situation up there, Mr. Scott?"

"I'm going out to do some more checking right now, Mr. Bing. I don't have much, but I can tell you one thing: William Carter, my predecessor on this case, is dead."

"Dead? What? Not—"

"Yeah. Dead, killed, murdered. Shot in the back. Does that help you think of anything else you could tell me about this mess?"

"Shot! Good Lord!" Then silence for a few seconds. "No, I'm sorry, Mr. Scott. There's nothing else." Then, "Shot. . . " he said again.

"O.K., then. O.K., Mr. Bing, I'll keep in touch with you. I'm afraid I don't have anything else definite, but I'll call you as soon as I do. I'll try to phone tomorrow, anyhow, one way or another."

"Well," he hesitated, "all right. You know my instructions."

"Sure."

"Please phone as soon as you can, Mr. Scott."

"I will." I hung up.

I sat thinking for about a minute, then stopped thinking about *that* and called another cab and had it sent to the Desert Inn. I was still going around in circles, and this one led right back to the courthouse.

This time I went clear up to the top and into the county clerk's office. I walked up to the wide counter and while I waited for the middle-aged lady with a well-fed and jovial appearance to finish making entries on a form at one of several desks behind the counter, two young couples came in behind me.

The lady finished scribbling and walked up to me. I nodded toward the four others and said, "I can wait. I'm just looking for information."

She smiled at the young people and said to them, "Just fill out one of these forms."

One of the men, a young, dark-haired fellow about twenty-two, grinned stiffly and reached convulsively for a pen in his coat pocket. He picked up one of the printed forms, "Information for Marriage License," which were spread along the counter.

I showed the lady my investigator's license, explained that I was from Los Angeles, and said, "I'd appreciate it if you'd check, when you have time, and see if there's an application for the marriage of Victor Dante and Isabel Ellis, or Isabel Bing, on file here."

She nodded. Apparently only two of the young people were getting married and the other two were witnesses. The nervous, dark-haired fellow swallowed and said, "Uh," and pushed the form across the counter. The tall blonde with him presented another form. My pleasant lady nodded to me, took the papers, and went to a typewriter. Soon she was back before the four young people and had the bride and groom sign some larger forms.

"That will be five dollars," she said.

The dark-haired one moved convulsively again and managed to come up with five dollars. "Let's get this over with," he mumbled. The blonde squeezed his arm hard. "Raise your right hands," the lady said. They did so and she asked them if they swore that all statements were true and so on.

"Yes," said the blonde.

"I guess so, sure," said her husband-to-be.

The jovial-looking lady said, "We wish you a great deal of happiness and it's just down the hall, the second door."

The four of them went out. I hoped they didn't wind up in the rest room.

In a few minutes, after checking the files, the lady was back in front of me. "Here you are," she said. "There is no record of an Isabel Ellis or an Isabel Bing. Mr. Dante was married here by Judge Orton on January third."

I needed a cigarette at this point so I lit one and asked, "Whom *did* he marry?"

"It's right here." She showed me on the marriage application. "Victor Dante and Crystal Claire."

I dropped my brand-new cigarette and stepped on it. I looked at the application. It was there, all right, just as she'd said. I told her, "Thanks. Thanks very much. I'd like this information and a copy of the marriage certificate if it's available."

She smiled. "Surely. You can get a photostatic copy of the certificate at the county recorder's office."

I thanked her and left. The four young people were already going down the stairs ahead of me. Holy vows had been made, and let no man put them asunder.

When I got back to my room at the Desert Inn I draped my coat over a chair, unstrapped my holster, and stuck it, gun and all, under the bedspread and pillow, then flopped on the bed to look over the stuff I'd accumulated.

All I knew from looking at the Nevada marriage application was that this Crystal Claire was twenty-six years old, this was her first marriage, and she

70

resided in the City of Las Vegas, County of Clark. About Dante I learned that he was thirty-six years old, marrying for the second time, his first wife was deceased, and he resided in the City of Las Vegas, County of Clark. And that was all except that the application had been sworn and subscribed on January 3, 1951, and the license had been issued the same day. They'd been married, all right. I'd seen the marriage certificate and copied the information from it.

I noted that January 3, the marriage date, was almost a month from December 6, the date on which Isabel Bing-Ellis-Dante-Smutch or whatever had sold her house and then apparently vanished. That sure did me a lot of good.

I shook my head. Right now the only thing I was sure of was that I wasn't sure of anything. But obviously I had to find out if the lovely who had fainted was my client's daughter. Well, at least I knew what to look for. Also, if there were some way I could get her fingerprints, I'd know for sure. That seemed to sum it up: fingerprints or fanny.

I tossed a coin and it came up just the way I'd hoped it would, and that settled that, but how did I go about it? It just wouldn't do to rush up to her and say, "Ah, there you are, Mrs. Dante. What ho! I say, old girl, would you swish off your bloomers and give me a bally old squint at your fanny?" No, that wouldn't do at all.

I needed a feminine viewpoint, and all these ideas running through my mind had made me want to see Colleen again, anyway. I picked up the phone and gave her a ring.

"Hello." It was that cute, crackly little voice again, and I could almost see her misty-eyed, innocent face. I could almost see more than that.

"How's my Irish Colleen, Mrs. Shawn?"

"Shell?"

"Sure it's Shell. Who else have you got calling you?"

She laughed. "Jealous? Nobody important, Shell. I missed you at lunch. Where were you?"

"In bed. I missed you, too."

She laughed again. "You must have gone to bed late. What were you up to?"

"Oh, I—" I shut up fast. I sure as hell couldn't tell her that. "I was investigating things. I'm still a detective."

"Shell," she said softly, "it is good to hear you talk. I was worried, honest. After last night—you know. Are you still in trouble with whoever. . . did that?"

"Yeah. I'm O.K., though. You can keep on worrying about me if you like. I don't mind at all."

"You looked so sort of grim when you got out at the Inferno last night. Oh! You weren't mixed up in *that* thing, were you?"

71

"What thing?"

"Some sort of a riot at the Inferno, I guess. Crazy man throwing money around like water, and a whole load of people ran out and fell down in the street or something. Everybody's talking about it."

"Uh. . . they are?"

"I should say so. Haven't you heard?"

"Yeah, I think I did hear something about it. Say, Colleen." It seemed time to change the subject. "I need some help. You know Victor Dante?"

"Know of him. I don't know him personally."

"You know his wife?"

"No, why?"

"Well—" I stopped again. This was a rather ticklish little question. "Tell me, Colleen. When you gals go out for a dip in the pool at the hotel here, where do you change?"

"In our own rooms. What in the world—"

"No sort of community bathhouse or dressing rooms?"

"No. Shell, tell me, why would that interest you?"

"Look, how about this? Meet me here or somewhere for a drink. I need a woman's viewpoint on a little problem."

"How about the bar in fifteen minutes?"

I would have much preferred my room, but the bar would have to do. I was going out later, anyway, and if I had to hide in my room all the time, I might as well give up and go back to Los Angeles.

"O.K.," I said. "See you down there."

"'By, Shell."

I hung up. She said fifteen minutes, and nine times out of ten when a woman says fifteen minutes she means an hour. If I went down now I'd probably be plastered by the time she arrived. I might blurt out exactly what I wanted to talk to her about and it could be that Colleen wouldn't cotton to the kind of thoughts I think. Particularly when I pointed out Mrs. Dante to her, if we could find her, and she noticed that cute little— Damn! There I went again.

I walked over to the window and looked down at the front of the hotel. It looked as if even more people had arrived for Helldorado today, because a steady stream of cars rolled up and down the highway, and in front of the hotel people were standing and laughing and horsing around, some of them in Western garb. There was a lot of horseplay, even more than I'd noticed yesterday. Helldorado was gathering momentum, rolling faster, and more liquor was being drunk and more hell being raised. Mix me another, and anything goes.

Even in the hotel there was a near bedlam. I could hear whoops and hollers in the hall outside my door, guys yelling hoarsely back and forth.

72

Down below a taxi drove up and six men climbed out, all of them sporting beards two or more inches long. I wondered who'd won the beard-growing contest.

About ten minutes had gone by since I'd phoned Colleen, and the noise was growing outside now. Then somebody banged away with a will on the door. Damn fools. I didn't care if they had fun, but they could leave me out of it. I was in no mood for any of the Helldorado horseplay right now.

They banged again like they were going to bust the door down. I walked over, unlocked the door, and swung it open.

There were three guys in the hall outside my door. Three cowboys. All dressed up in cute little cowboy suits and having a hell of a good time. Three clowns. They seemed to be about half drunk, and they were whooping and yelling and waving toy guns at me, and one guy was carrying a rope or lariat with a hangman's noose in one end. That was a laugh. A hangman's noose. What would the crazy characters in this town think of next?

12

YES, SIR, that was sure a clever old noose, but I got only a quick glimpse of all that happiness and right then one of the big ugly men stuck his little toy gun up in my kisser and I came very close to throwing up. Because that was no toy, that was sure enough no toy. Things happened fast after that. I started to slam the door but a foot was in the way and the first guy gave me a stiff arm in the face. I staggered back, started to jump toward the bed and my gun, out of sight under the pillow, and then didn't even wiggle. The guy who'd shoved me was a red-faced character with big pink ears, and he had a gun four feet from me, and there were two other guns in two other fists, which made three real guns pointing at me. I was the center of attention again.

And now I recognized the big-eared guy and the other two. The one farthest away from me, who had been half hidden by others in that first quick look I got at them, was naturally the sadistic blighter who'd started going around with me at the Pelican: Lloyd something or other, the bartender had told me. So Lloyd *had* seen me. The others were the two who had first started with bushy-haired Lloyd into the crowd at the Inferno after me last night.

I stood still when I'd caught my balance, but I said, "You guys nuts? You can't pull anything in here."

"Shut up!" Big Ears snapped at me. "Keep it shut." He moved around behind me. I started to turn so I could keep an eye on him. I hated the thought of getting a gun butt on my skull. But Lloyd stepped up in front of me and wiggled his gun at my face, the big vein bulging in his brown forehead.

"You just hold still, Scott, or you'll get this mixed up with your teeth, Scott," he singsonged. "Hold it steady and you won't get hurt. Honest."

He lied.

While I was still wondering about the guy behind me and looking at the hard metal of Lloyd's big .45 automatic, it happened. I didn't hear a thing; there was just the now familiar explosion inside my head.

There was a cottony taste in my mouth and I was on something soft. I was afraid to open my eyes; I was afraid that soft stuff might be a cloud. And my head hurt like blazes as I remembered what had happened and I knew my head shouldn't hurt if I were dead, and I started peeling open my eyes, a fraction of an inch at a time.

Finally they were open. I was still in my room and on the bed. Maybe— But there was no maybe about it. The three goons were looking at me, and I might possibly have jumped up yelling and killed them except that my hands were tied behind my back, and that cottony taste in my mouth was from a big wad of cloth stuffed between my teeth for a gag, and I felt absolutely horrible. I could feel something across the front of my face, too, but I couldn't tell what it was.

The three guys grinned and made some cracks about my being cute, and then I noticed something peculiar. When they'd come in they'd all been completely outfitted in the spirit of Helldorado days: cowboy Stetsons, shirts, neckerchiefs, jackets, and chaps. There were pieces missing now. Lloyd had no Stetson or neckerchief; Big Ears didn't have any colorful jacket; and the other guy was minus his chaps.

I'd been wondering how the devil these guys figured they could pull anything in the Desert Inn, but all of a sudden when I looked at them my stomach felt cold and slimy because now I knew what they were going to do. I bent my head down and took a look at Shell Scott, still the Cactus Kid. I was a real cowboy now, dressed up in all their missing articles, with my mouth gagged and something else looped around my neck and hanging down on my chest—a foot-square, hand-lettered sign that I couldn't read—and my hands bound behind me.

Lloyd was twirling that laughable noose in his hands, and I knew what they were going to do. They were simply going to walk me right out of here and hang me.

I started to yell at them that they must be out of their minds, that they couldn't possibly get away with such a crazy, idiotic scheme as this one, but all I got out was a strangled "Mmmmph!" through the gag and they whooped and hollered because I was so funny.

Lloyd said, "How you feel, Scott, how you feel? You only been out five minutes. Think you can walk? Navigate? Git up, podner, git on yore hoss." And they whooped and yelped some more, but I failed to see the humor in the situation.

Lloyd meant it, though, when he told me to get up. He came to the bed and bent over me and I tried to kick him in his big teeth and missed and he even thought that was funny. They hauled me to my feet, and my feet weren't tied. For two seconds the thought skittered in my mind that there might be a chance I could run for it, but it was for only two seconds because that was the length of time it took Lloyd to toss the rope over my neck and jam the thirteen turns of a hangman's knot tight up against my Adam's apple.

I wanted that gag out of my mouth so I could tell him to take it easy; already I could feel the strain in breathing because of the tightness of that loop, and I knew, even if he didn't, that a man doesn't have to swing free to hang himself—that he can hang from a doorknob or a bedpost or a noose in a man's hands. And if Lloyd didn't know how quickly a man becomes unconscious when the neck arteries and veins can't carry blood between the heart and brain, then he had a bad memory.

He played out five or six feet of the rope and pulled me after him, and I could feel Big Ears hauling away on the rope attached to my hands behind me. That rope was looped a time or two around my wrists, but it didn't end there and Big Ears wasn't holding it at my wrists. Like Lloyd, he'd played out a few feet of the line and held it a couple of yards behind me. They had me fixed so that I couldn't even run *toward* Lloyd. I couldn't even move enough to kick the bastards, and my arms were pulled out and up behind my back till I was afraid they'd pop out of place at the shoulders. I was stretched in between them as Lloyd went to the door, and I mean *stretched,* so I couldn't possibly run.

Before Lloyd opened the door he said to the other two men, "Now, don't screw this up, you guys." He looked from one to the other of them coldly. "Remember, this is a gag; it's gotta go smooth. Don't act nervous. If you gotta, then talk to people, but only if you gotta, and let's get him outta here as fast as we can. But play it smart. You don't have to worry about him; he can't say a thing."

He looked at me then and gave a tug on the rope. "How *you* like getting choked, Scott?" Then, just before we left the room, he said the words that were to be the last I'd ever hear him say to me in this lifetime. "Scott," he said happily, "we're gonna kill you. Murder you. I guess you know you're dead. You should have listened to my advice."

Sort of an epitaph: You should have listened.

Lloyd opened the door and started out, and as we passed the dresser I got a quick glance at the procession in the mirror: noose around my neck leading forward to Lloyd, me all dressed up pretty, then rope around my hands leading back to Big Ears. It was almost as if they were leading a burro or a jackass. And in that flashing glimpse into the mirror I saw what was across my face. A black bandanna was stretched over my nose and mouth, hanging down below my chin, then passed around my face and tied in back. The Stetson was jammed down on my ears, and about all that was visible of me were my eyes and eyebrows, and the rest of me was dressed as I'd never been dressed before. Not even God would have recognized me.

We went out the door, with them still gaily waving their guns, and no matter how silly I'd thought this was before, I didn't think it was silly now. Because they could get away with it. They'd planned it all before they came, they'd been ready, and now we were on our way. And I knew that downtown and even here on the Strip scenes similar to this were going on, the only difference being that this was a little more elaborate than most. Men had been thrown into Helldorado jail for no reason at all; other men were waving guns at the sky; kids played cops and robbers and shot each other with cap pistols. Yeah, they could get away with it.

And, like that, we went out the door, and I heard it bang shut behind me, and we started down the hall. Me and my three clowns.

13

THE LOBBY was jammed. I was really scared now, and it seemed as if I caught a dozen impressions of the color and noise and activity all at once and grabbed onto them and held them as if I might never see anything like them again. I got a flash of a woman's face as she laughed, a beautiful face with flashing white teeth and the tip of a red tongue curling. In the confused blur of men's suits and women's cocktail dresses and sports outfits, there were several Western outfits similar to mine, plus a lot of blue jeans and bright shirts. And everybody seemed to be laughing or smiling. This was the same feverish having fun intensity I'd noticed in the Inferno last night, only now it seemed even gayer and brighter and better.

There were other guys with guns, and one little brat about five or six years old, in a Hopalong Cassidy set of junior cowboy togs, held a water pistol in his right hand and squirted a stream of water across the lobby.

I caught all that in a flash as we got to the bottom of the stairs and then we were right out in the lobby passing the desk on our right and people caught sight of us. I thought, Maybe, maybe here's where these smart bastards get theirs, but people started grinning and laughing. They pointed and nudged each other and some of the goddamn fools roared their heads off.

78

They were dying laughing; this was a scream. Our procession was stalled momentarily as a group came past us and a couple of other guys came up to offer all four of us comedians a drink, and one fat old guy about fifty-five and drunk as a lord reeled up alongside me with tears streaming from his eyes.

He pointed at the sign I hadn't been able to read on my chest and his big belly jiggled. *"Waaaahh!"* he roared. "Hoss thief!" Then he haw-hawed for a couple of seconds and gurgled, "What you gonna do with him?"

Lloyd, with a tight grip on the rope that was choking hell out of me, answered happily, "Gonna hang him."

The fat guy couldn't stand it. He whooped and roared and doubled over. *"Hang him!"* he yelped in hysterics. "Oooohhh, boy! That's good!"

Yeah, it was good. It was so good I wanted to kick the old bastard square in his manhood.

And then I saw Colleen Shawn.

She was standing right at the edge of the lobby with her back to the casino, and a short, dark jacket draped over her shoulders, and I knew she was the only person in this whole building who might recognize me and the trouble I was in, and, some way or any way, help me. And she looked at us, and looked straight at me, and looked away.

But she was still looking, looking all around her with a worried expression on her lovely face, and I knew she was looking for me. She was looking for me, but she'd looked right at me and it hadn't meant a thing.

I could feel sweat on my forehead and under the black mask that covered up my face, and I didn't know what I could do, but I was ready to try anything.

The fat guy clapped me on the shoulder and said, still giggling, "What's your name? You're terrific."

I wanted to tell him my name was mud, but I couldn't get anything out but muffled mmmmphs. I mmmmphed as loud as I could, hoping this stupid drunk would catch on, but Lloyd caught on instead and yanked hard on the rope and I could feel my face getting red.

And right then in about five seconds a whole mess of things happened, bang, bang, bang, like that. A middle-aged woman in a blue dress said, "Oh, you're hurting him," and I mentally agreed with her, and the fat character went off into hysterics again right beside me, and the little delinquent cretin sprayed his water pistol at us, and I had an idea.

I had an idea how I could let Colleen know, and right at that moment she turned her back on me and started to go back into the casino, and I said it's now or never and lunged toward the fat Laughing Boy and felt that goddamn noose tightening on my throat as I butted him and butted him again with my head.

He stopped laughing and sputtered and gasped, but the big floppy Stetson toppled off that stupid, blond-white, stand-up hair of mine and fell to the floor, and Lloyd said, "Son of a—" and stopped, and the little delinquent looked up at me and his stupid little mouth dropped open.

Colleen was walking away and I thought, For Christ's sake, stop, woman, but she took another step as Lloyd yanked again and Big Ears jerked from behind, and then the little water-pistol kid, still gaping at me, shut his mouth, opened it, and staring at my whitish hair he screamed, "Mommy, they're killing *Hoppy!* They're gonna *bang* him!" and I thought, You should have your mouth washed out with soap, but then I loved him.

Because that high-pitched yelp made a couple of dozen people swing their heads around at us and one of them was Colleen. She looked back over her shoulder and at first there was nothing in her face except mild curiosity, and then she saw me in a tug of war with two guys, and I wiggled my eyebrows at her, and my scalp and nose and navel, and she saw Lloyd grab the Stetson and shove it down on my head again, but not before she knew.

I could hardly see her now because the rope was twisting me and damn near cutting off my wind, but I knew this was a break, better than no break at all, and I was going to kiss that lovable little child if I lived; I was going to slobber all over him disgustingly and I'd buy him Hoppy's own gun, and Hoppy's own horse—hell, I'd buy him Hoppy.

Our procession had been stalled for no more than half a minute and now we were under way again. I bulged the muscles in my neck as tight as I could because I was getting black spots in front of my eyes, and as we moved and started out the door, the Hopalong fan's mother said, "That's not Hoppy, darling; that's just a nice man. They're playing a game." And Colleen ran right up to us and past us and away somewhere. I couldn't turn around to watch her go, but I knew it was Colleen.

We went through the main entrance, then turned left under the redwood-roofed portico before which the cars drive up and unload. We were a twelve-foot procession with Lloyd up front and the third man running interference beside him, then rope and me, then rope and Big Ears. Cars were parked out front and over at the left, where we were heading, and probably there was a car up ahead waiting for me. I was walking along with the boys, my eyesight fairly good now, but still having trouble breathing.

It was dusk that would soon be dark. Probably Lloyd and the others had planned it that way, but there was still barely enough light left so that people out front could see us and point and get their kicks. It was going out of me now—all the temporary exhilaration I'd felt when Colleen had recognized me after I'd made that last attempt to cross these guys. I'd shot my bolt, and there wasn't anything else I could try. But I knew if I had my hands on

Lloyd's throat now, I wouldn't stop choking him till his face was blue and he was dead.

We reached the edge of the building and started to step into the asphalt drive when three more people came around the building's edge and went through the same old tired routine. They pointed and laughed and came up close to us, and one of them, a woman, was screaming, "Horse thief, horse thief," and laughing a tight, shrill, almost hysterical laugh, and it was Colleen.

She laughed in Lloyd's face and the face of the other man by him and came right up to me choking and laughing and sobbing, and then I felt her hand behind me as she slashed with a knife and cut me with the keen blade, ripped the knife into my skin and tore the flesh to the bone as she sliced at the ropes, but the ropes came free. I grabbed the knife and held it for a fraction of a second while the warm blood streamed down over it and I felt the pain, and I knew I had them now, knew it even as the man behind me felt the rope go slack in his hands and let out a startled yell. I knew it as surely as I ever knew anything in my life, and I didn't even feel as if I had to hurry.

Colleen was gone as soon as I grabbed the knife, and as Big Ears yelled behind me Lloyd knew something was wrong and jerked sharply on the rope around my neck. I went right along with it as the man on Lloyd's left swung around to face me, and felt as if I were floating toward them even though I knew my legs were driving me.

It had taken no more than half a second from the time the rope slipped free and Lloyd heard the shout, but he was swinging around as I reached him, his gun coming up, and I squeezed the knife tight in my right hand and whipped my hand up fast from my side, slashing up at him, and I hit his belly with the knife and jammed it up to the hilt inside him. His gasp mingled with the curse of the other man raising his gun and chopping it around at me, and I threw up my left hand and caught the swinging gun barrel against the flesh of my arm. With my left arm up to catch the blow, I crossed my right arm in front of my stomach, my hand stretched out stiff and quivering, and whipped it up fast, aiming for the spot right underneath his nose. Because I wasn't fooling with this bastard, not now I wasn't, and I swung my hand up as hard and fast as I could, with all the power I could get behind it, and I felt the edge of my palm smash under his nose and knew that splinters of bone were flying into the darkness of his brain, and that he was dead before he fell.

I swung around, hoping the other guy wasn't behind me, right on top of me, but he was gone. Big Ears had liked it while things were going his way, but now I could hear feet slapping as somebody ran. The whole mess here hadn't taken more than a few seconds after I'd got the knife, and that was probably Big Ears just now getting under way as I heard the dead man's head smack against the pavement when he fell behind my back.

Lloyd was hunched over on his knees, groaning and cursing, so he was still alive. I don't know what I'd have done then if some people from the front of the hotel hadn't come over slowly, attracted by the scuffle. I jerked the rope from around my neck and dropped it. I didn't want strangers talking to me now, and I didn't care to see Lieutenant Hawkins, so I ran. I ran around to the back of the Desert Inn. I knew that nobody except Colleen knew who the funny "hoss thief" had been, so out of sight of anybody from the hotel I took off the chaps and neckerchief and jacket, pulled off the mask that had covered my face, and took the gag out of my mouth. I found a faucet outside one of the cottages and quickly washed the blood off my hands.

I went into the Desert Inn the back way, past the figure-eight swimming pool, stopping long enough in the light from the doorway to make sure my shirt and trousers didn't show any telltale spots of red. There was a small streak across the front of my shirt, but otherwise I seemed presentable enough. Most of what blood there was had been on the Western clothes I'd left in back.

I stuck my hands into my pockets and went in. I went in fast and crossed to the stairs in a hurry, because I wanted to get up to my room and my gun before any commotion broke loose in the hotel, because the two goons had undoubtedly been found by now. I wanted to get to my room and out of it again before anybody else came calling; I wanted to get something on my still bleeding hands; and I wanted to find Colleen and be sure she was all right.

14

NOBODY looked at me as I crossed the lobby. Word hadn't seeped inside this soon, and everybody seemed to be having too much fun to pay a lot of attention if it had. I went up the stairs and down the hall to my room. The door was unlocked and pulled shut as we'd left it, and by all the rules nobody should be in there. I wasn't convinced, though, and I made as little noise as I could when I put my hand on the knob and twisted it slowly, then threw the door open so hard that it swung around and banged against the wall.

From the doorway I looked around the room fast, ready to run if I had to, but this time I wouldn't have to run. The room was empty. I went inside, straight to the bed, and looked under the pillow. My .38 was still there, and I grabbed it before I did anything else. Then I got a towel, took it back to the door, and wiped my blood from the outside knob before I shut it again and locked it.

My right hand was practically untouched except for a small gash on my wrist where the ropes had been; most of the blood had come from my left hand and wrist, still bleeding. My wrist was the worst, where Colleen had slashed deeply through to the bone, but in her haste she'd sliced a piece out of my thumb and the knife had continued down to cut across the inside of all four fingers, which had been outside, away from my back. I held the towel around my left hand while I phoned Colleen's room. She didn't answer.

I let the phone ring for a while, then hung up and fixed my hands. I made a fast job of it with gauze and tape, hurried into a clean shirt and gray gabardine suit from my bag, strapped on my gun, and went out.

I was worried about Colleen, but I wasn't going to stick in my room phoning her. That room wasn't much good to me any more; not with my name on the hotel register and Dante's gunmen getting bold enough to walk right inside and grab me. I walked down to the hallway on the main floor and up it to Colleen's room. I knocked, and when there wasn't any answer I tried the door, but it was locked.

I wanted to hang around a while and see if Colleen showed up, but I didn't want to have my bare face sticking right out in the open. And, too, I wanted to sit in someplace quiet for a while and gather my thoughts, try to make sense of this mess. I was not in very good mental shape right at this moment, and physically I was a six-foot-two ache. The cuts weren't so bad, though they burned, but I could feel a lot of bruises on me and the worst of all was my head. If I'd had the chance, I'd have given the thing away. Every time my heart beat, the inside of my head throbbed as if it were beating instead of my heart. It was like migraine without the dizziness.

I walked back to the end of the hall again and looked out into the lobby. Everything seemed to be going on normally. Just beyond the desk, before you go into the casino, there's a flight of stairs that leads up into the Sky Room Cocktail Lounge, clear up at the top of the Desert Inn. There was a spot where I could wait in about as much safety as seemed left to me in this town, and where I could also have a drink. Having a drink seemed like the best idea I'd had for the last two or three days. Having several drinks seemed like an even better idea. That's what I'd do about those aches and pains: I'd anesthetize myself.

I walked past the desk and headed for the stairs, and out in the open again I felt like a naked man captured by the Society for the Suppression of Vice and Everything, but nothing happened and I made it up the stairs, in past the stools in front of the black piano inside the lounge's entrance, and around to the far side of the oval bar. I sat with my back to the huge mirror that covers the whole wall, where I could watch the entrance, and ordered a double bourbon and water. The bartender glanced at my taped fingers but didn't say anything. He brought the drink. It was gone in no time. I had another. Nothing happened while I drank the second one; no bombs went off, nobody shot at me, nobody lassoed me, no lightning struck me. I had another.

Before I finished that one I knew what my next move would be. I hadn't yet done what I'd started out to do at the very beginning of this case: *talk* to

84

Lorraine Mandel. I wasn't about to bust in on Victor Dante again, not just to ask questions, but I did want to make conversation with Lorraine, because she might be able to give me some of the missing pieces. She definitely seemed like the best place for me to pick up more information if she were willing to talk and knew anything that would help me, but the problem was how to get to her. I finished my third double and ordered another drink.

"Single this time," I told the bartender. "Single little drink." He brought the highball.

I was feeling better and worse at the same time. Maybe I *did* have migraine. My head wasn't hurting so much, but I was getting some dizziness. And here I was in Las Vegas' Helldorado, and damn near everybody seemed to be having fun but me. I started feeling sorry for myself. No fair, no fair at all. Everybody having fun. All I was doing was trying to keep from getting killed. I considered that as the bourbon oozed into my blood stream.

"Bartender, little single. One little drinkie."

I got the drink. It had been night outside for quite a while now and I could look across the bar and out the wide windows and down the Strip to the lights of the night clubs, and cars moving up and down the highway. Joe E. Lewis was packing them in at El Rancho Vegas; Arthur Lee Simpkins was knocking them dead at the Flamingo; Carl Ravazza was here in the Painted Desert Room of the Desert Inn. And in the Sky Room: me. All alone.

I phoned Colleen's room several times with no luck, then mapped my campaign for seeing Lorraine Mandel. I know I couldn't run laughing into the Inferno and ask for her, and she was undoubtedly slaying them in the floor shows there, anyway. But I had a vague, possibly bourbon-inspired plan of what I could do. That little hanging party that went awry earlier had given me an idea.

I ordered one last drink while I examined the idea, then grabbed a cab and had myself driven downtown to Fremont Street. People were whooping it up and having their kicks as I pushed through them and went into a store where all sorts of costumes were rented and sold and a lot of knick-knacks and gadgets were on display. I went inside exhaling fumes of bourbon. I looked around for a few minutes, then got the clerk, a young gal about nineteen, and pointed to a set of brightly colored clothes.

"Miss. Like to rent that and put it on here."

"Sure. In back. You want the Mexican outfit?"

"That's the one." It was the one. Starting from the top, there was a big, floppy, black sombrero with a brim that would hide part of my face. Then there was a scarlet jacket covered with intricate needlework and silver spangles, and a pair of flaring trousers of black cloth with silver stitching up the outsides of the pants legs. The girl got the stuff and I changed into it in back, then bought a brightly colored serape to go over my shoulders.

85

I took a look at myself in a mirror, and I looked like a rainbow, but there was still my face staring out at me from under the floppy brim of the hat. This wouldn't do—not if I were going to barge right into the Inferno. Then on a table I saw some gadgets that gave me another idea. Like two or three of the stores on Fremont Street, this one had quite a collection of jokes and novelties: imitation ink blots, leaking or "dribble" glasses, marked cards. Cute things like that. But there were two disgusting little items side by side among all the rest that might solve my problem. One of them was called "Goofy Teeth" and the other had no name because there was probably no name gruesome enough to describe it. It was a pair of eyes. Bulbous, white, red-veined eyes with brilliant blue half-inch circles painted around the pupils, and the pupils were quarter-inch holes through which your own eyes could look out. There was a curved metal band to fit over the wearer's nose, and attached were ghastly bulging eyes.

If you have ever seen a man wearing a pair of those eyes over his own, and a set of fanglike, twisted Goofy Teeth jutting from under his upper lip, then you know that there is absolutely nothing more hideous that can ever happen to that man's face. It happened to mine.

I bought the teeth and eyes, slipped them on in front of the mirror, and yanked them off before they scared me while the little clerk laughed and laughed.

"Thanks," I told her. "Pretty awful, huh?"

"Pretty awful. You going to a party?"

"Yeah. You got a black eyebrow pencil somewhere?"

She squinted at me curiously, but she came up with the pencil. I blacked my eyebrows with it after she told me to go ahead and ruin the pencil if I wanted to, then I tried the eyes and teeth again. It was even worse than before.

But I paid the girl and left with her laughter still bubbling behind me. I left my own clothes in the store, saying I'd pick them up later. I had my gun strapped across my chest under the scarlet jacket, and my teeth and eyes in the jacket's pocket. The floppy sombrero rested on my head, the serape was draped over my shoulders, and I was one God-awful mess. I'd gone into the shop as a fairly respectable Sheldon Scott, Los Angeles private detective; now I was Señor Scott, the private *ojo*.

I had another quick drink to keep my courage up, then caught a cab and got out in front of the Inferno. People still streamed in and out of the Devil's mouth, and I pulled the floppy sombrero down over my face, slipped in my teeth, popped on my eyes, and went in.

86

15

OURBON bubbled pleasantly inside me and I was feeling a mite dizzy. It occurred to me that, just possibly, Señor Scott, the private *ojo*, was more than a bit plastered. But I had to find my Sweet Lorraine, and after all the trouble I was going to, she'd better be ready to talk. I went into the Devil's Room wishing I had some of the instruments of torture depicted on its walls. Say a whip or a club or a thumb screw. Then if she wouldn't talk I could whip it out of her or beat it out of her or use the thumb screw on her. I hunched over and headed for the dining room.

Music was blaring from the room; the last floor show was on. What the hell did I do now? I slipped inside the door and waited among the tables at the back of the room. Nobody noticed me because everybody was watching the show, and because the big room was in darkness except for the stage. As long as the club lights were out I was O.K., but if they suddenly came on there was a chance I'd feel foolish. With the stage on my left, I walked straight ahead to the far wall, stopped, and turned around. A tall brunette finished singing, bowed to the applause, then went backstage through a curtained archway at the side of the orchestra stand. Backstage was where I wanted, but I couldn't use the same route getting there that she'd used. There had to be another way to get there without climbing up on the stage in front of all these people. I kept peering through my quarter-inch holes till I saw, dimly, another door in the wall at the right of the stage. That probably led back where I wanted to go, and I was getting ready to wander over when the MC announced, "The star of our show: Lorraine," and she came on.

She was wearing a dark blue evening gown that clung to her white skin. That black hair was loose down her back and she was smiling as she moved over the polished floor. This was no fire dance, but I had an idea it would be good because she was still the full-breasted and wide-hipped wanton I remembered from the Pelican. And remembered, too, from last night. I wanted to watch, but it seemed a good time for me to try that door while all the guests were staring at the shapely body gliding over the dance floor.

I walked to the wall and turned the knob on the door, and it opened. I went on through and pulled the door shut behind me. I was in a short hallway much like the one I'd been in at the Pelican, except that at my left, behind the stage, a flight of stairs led up to what were probably dressing rooms above. I moved to my left, to a spot a few yards from the archway through which Lorraine would come when her act was finished, and waited in the dim light from overhead bulbs.

The music ended and there was a loud burst of applause that hurt my head, then Lorraine came through the archway, turned around with her back to me, and waited. She had on a lot more clothing than she used in her fire dance, but the whole outfit couldn't have weighed more than a few ounces, and for some reason that pleased me.

I went "Psst!" at her, but apparently she didn't hear me. The applause kept up out front and she went back to bow again. I found myself wishing I were ringside so I could applaud and yell for more like the rest, and watch her bow.

Then she was back.

"Psst," I said. "Pssssst!"

She turned around just as she started up the flight of steps to the dressing rooms and she looked straight at me. I'd forgotten temporarily about the way I must look, serape and teeth and eyes and all the rest, but Lorraine got it all at once as I caught her eye. The way I looked I must not only have caught her eye, but practically yanked it out.

Her eyes lit up like light bulbs and I thought she was going to scream. There is a certain slang expression meaning "look at" in a certain startled manner. It is "eyeball," and there is no word that better describes what Lorraine did to me. She eyeballed me till I thought her eyeballs were going to go *spoc* and jump clear across ten feet at me. I thought they were going to fly across space like bumblebees and smack me in the kisser.

She looked horrified, startled, incredulous, and nauseated, not by turns but all at once. She sucked in her breath with a little squeaking sound and stood staring at me. She was paralyzed and squeaking, and I suddenly realized what was the matter.

I pawed at my face and got my ghoulish eyes and teeth off and said cleverly, "Lorraine. It's me!"

She stopped making noises but her mouth dropped open.

I pushed my sombrero back on my head and said, "It's only me. I won't hurt you. C'mere."

Some of the expressions faded from her face till all that was left was a kind of pained horror. "You!" she said.

People were still applauding like mad out front, but they were missing the best part of the show. The best part of the show is always backstage, anyway. And I had an idea they could applaud till their hands were pulpy and Lorraine wouldn't take another call. I don't think she could have made it. She was leaning against the wall with one hand on her breast and her mouth still open and sucking in air. She looked too weak to climb the stairs and, looking at her skimpy costume, I decided I'd carry her.

She stared at me, recognizable now, and she said, "Well, yippee-ti-yo. Are you cracking up, Dad? What happened?"

"Couldn't just walk in. Told you last night. Got to talk to you."

"For all I knew, you were dead. Are you? You look like something fresh from an old grave."

"Look. Can't stand here. Got to talk to you."

She sighed hugely, blew air out of her mouth, puffing her cheeks, and said, "Come on. I want to get a good look at you."

She turned and went up the stairs with me right behind her. When she took that good look she wanted at me, we'd be even. At the top of the steps we went into the first dressing room and she shut the door, locked it, and leaned back against it.

She looked at me some more, shaking her head. "Don't you ever do anything like that to me again," she said. She put a hand over her heart and seemed surprised to find that all she had on was a gauzy bra and an abbreviated pair of shorts. I wasn't surprised; I'd known it all the time.

"I need a drink," I said.

"You need a drink." She grabbed a dressing gown off a hook and squeezed into it. "I need half a dozen after that. I thought you were something that had come to get me. What are you doing here, anyway?"

I grinned at her, "Why, Lorraine. It's such a nice night that I thought—"

"Now, wait a minute," she said quickly, but smiling. "You didn't creep back here in that getup just to ask me out in the balmy night air again.

Not after the ruckus you had with Dante here last night. Now, what *do* you want?"

I said, "Last night, downstairs before I started the ball rolling, you said you'd like to help me. You mean it?"

"I guess so. I still don't know what you were talking about. But look, we can't stay here. How about my room?"

"You through with the show?"

"Yes. And we can't get a drink up here. I think I'll die if I don't get a drink." She peered at me. "You know, I had you set as a big, rough-looking guy. Not a bad-looking guy at all. A guy I could kind of go for, all things considered." She shook her head. "But I don't think you'll ever look quite the same to me again. I'll always see you plucking out your eyes."

"I promise not to do it again. And your room's fine, but I'll have to get through the crowd without being recognized."

"We can make it, all right," she said. "You can wear your. . . Ugh. Just don't look at me."

She stepped to a folding screen, did highly interesting things behind it, then stepped out fully dressed in a white blouse and brown skirt, and with spike-heeled shoes on her nylon-stockinged feet. She said, "We won't have to go through the crowd below. Come on."

I followed her out of the dressing room, down the hall to another door, then through it onto the second floor of the hotel and down the long corridor lined with rooms. She led me to 232 and unlocked the door, and we went inside.

She went straight to the phone and called room service for bourbon, ice, and ginger ale. Then she turned to me and smiled. "Well. . . " she said.

"Yeah," I said. "Well, uh. . . " It was fairly obvious that we were both remembering the same thing. We'd been pretty sad-looking people the last time we'd seen each other.

She said, "Well, what did you want to talk about?"

I'd gone to a lot of trouble to ask Lorraine some questions; it was time I started. I grinned at her. "Before—before we left the Inferno last night, I asked you some questions and you said you didn't know what I was talking about, remember?" She nodded, and I added, "I, uh, sort of forgot to bring the subject up again."

Her smile got wider, then it faded and she said, "I do remember. But you never did really explain what you meant. About your car, and that fellow getting killed."

She sprawled on the bed and I pulled a chair over near her and told her the whole thing. I made it short and fast, but got enough of it in so it would make sense to her if she didn't already know all of it. I made it pretty strong about Dante's wanting to kill me, and the part she might have played in causing Freddy's death, and also told her about Carter.

When I finished she sat quietly for a few moments, biting that sensually curved lower lip. Then she turned her blue eyes on me. "I didn't realize. . . " she said softly. "I honestly didn't. But if I could have had anything to do with that Freddy's getting killed—" She stopped, then went on, "I did tell Dante about seeing you in the limousine. It could have happened exactly the way you said."

There was a knock on the door and I was on my feet with my gun in my hand before whoever it was finished knocking.

Lorraine stared at the gun for a moment, then looked at me. "I guess you're not kidding," she said quietly.

"Baby, get it through your head once and for all. This is nothing to kid about."

She nodded and went to the door. I stood aside, but it was only the bell-hop with the liquor. Lorraine took care of him, then locked the door and carried the bottles to the dresser. She mixed two drinks, putting a splash of water in mine when I told her that was how I liked it, then gave me my drink and took a long swallow at hers.

Then she said, looking at me, "I'm sorry. I'm awfully sorry, Shell. What do you want to know?"

"First, why wouldn't you talk to me at the Pelican?"

"Dante. Victor Dante." She went over to the bed and curled up on it again. I swallowed part of my drink and I could tell that I'd already had plenty because it was turning to steam in my stomach. Lorraine sure looked terrific on that bed. She went on, "He came down just a little while before you showed up that night." She stopped, sighed, then said, "It was sure nice while it lasted." She waved a hand in an all-inclusive gesture. "Star billing here. Free room. Everything on the house like I worked for RFC. It's all for exactly what I'm not doing now: keeping my mouth shut."

"Dante set this up for you? To keep you quiet?" She nodded and I said, "Look, start at the beginning, with Isabel or Carter, and bring it right on up so I can get the picture as it happened." I could feel that bourbon taking hold and I wanted to hear whatever she had to say before it just didn't matter to me. Lorraine sure looked good on that bed. And, as I remembered, she *was* good.

Then she said something that sobered me a little. "I told you the truth before, Shell. I don't know this Isabel."

"You know Mrs. Dante?"

"Yes."

"Who is she?"

"Before they got married she was Crystal Claire."

"And who the hell is Crystal Claire?"

"Girl I worked with at the Pelican—my best friend there. We got along swell. She's the girl I talked to that detective, Carter, about."

I sighed and got up, finished my drink, and walked to the dresser. "Lorraine, do you mind if I mix another?"

She leaned forward and held her glass toward me. She smiled. "Fix two." I fixed them and took one to her.

"Sit here," she said. She patted the bed beside her. "You sure look awful. Take off your serape."

I took it off and sat down beside her as she scooted over to give me room. I said, "O.K., give it to me."

She grinned a lot and wiggled a little. I said, "What about this Crystal? What about everything?"

She kept smiling at first, but she started in. "I was in the show at the Pelican"—she paused and grinned at me—"and Crystal was a cigarette girl. Cute, too."

"I know. That's Dante's wife? Little blonde gal?"

"Uh-huh. She wasn't Dante's wife then, but he was hot for her. Hung around her a lot when he came down. He owns the Pelican, or most of it, and he came around regularly on the first and fifteenth of each month. Anyway, Crystal worked there a couple of months or so, and then one day she didn't show up."

"When was that, Lorraine? What day?"

She frowned. "Right at the first of the year. Second or third of January, I think. I don't remember exactly."

"O.K., go on."

"Well, there's nothing to tell until this detective showed up and asked me about some Isabel. I didn't know any Isabel—just like I told you, Shell—but he showed me a picture of her and it sure looked like Crystal."

That slowed me down for a minute. "Was it Crystal?"

"I'm not sure, but it was enough like her so that I mentioned it to Mr. Carter. He thanked me, asked a few questions about Crystal, and left."

"Who else at the Pelican knew Dante was—well, hot for Crystal?"

"Well," she said, frowning again, "probably nobody but me. They didn't bite each other in the club. And I might not have known except that Crystal and I got along so good and she told me. Probably I was the only one."

"Something else. Did you tell Carter about Dante's interest in this Crystal, and that Dante was from Vegas?"

"Yes, I did. Nobody told me not to. Why shouldn't I?"

And maybe that explained how Carter had wound up in Las Vegas. But it didn't explain why he'd wound up dead, I said, "O.K., what then?"

"Nothing till the night you showed up, Shell."

"Uh-huh. And when I busted in, Dante was in your dressing room. What was that all about?"

"Well, he was smooth, but he said he wanted me to star at the Inferno, and he also wanted to give me a thousand dollars. There was one little catch. I had to forget I'd ever seen that detective or heard of Crystal Claire. He said I'd have to keep my goddamned mouth shut." She giggled slightly. "That's what he said, my goddamned mouth." She paused, blinking her eyes. She spent ten seconds blinking and thinking and said, "Wanted me to go with him right away then, he did. In his car."

"Uh-huh. Think I saw the car. For a second. Why didn't you go back with him?"

"Thousand dollars? I should go? I had to get some clothes if I was coming up here. Didn't I?"

"Yes. You sure did." I guess she did, so she could make a good first impression. Only, as I remembered, with Lorraine it wasn't really the first impression that counted.

"So I did," she said. "And so I took the plane in the afternoon. Shell, fix me a drink."

"You got another show to do?"

"No more show. Only two shows, just did the last one." I fixed two more drinks.

She went on, "Golly, Shell, you can see how wonderful that sounded to me. I didn't know of anything wrong, and star billing at the Inferno in Las Vegas. . . ." She let it trail off and was quiet for a moment. "Guess that's over."

I said, "Lorraine, honey. Hate to say this, but there's a chance that's not all that's over if Dante finds out you've talked to me. There's been one murder already, besides Freddy." I thought about that a minute and added, "At least one murder."

Her face got sober and she pulled at her drink. The way she pulled at it, her face wasn't going to stay sober. Then she smiled at me and we sat on the bed and drank our highballs. It was getting a little wobbly in the room. Things were sort of rubbery and they didn't exactly stay put the way things should. We had another little drink and chatted gaily for a while. The bourbon crept up on us. I didn't learn a hell of a lot more. I liked Lorraine's long black hair better loose the way it was now than in a bun, I decided. And I liked that full lower lip, and the pouting mouth and impudent eyes and the nose that was too small for her face.

Finally I said, "Dante came down first and fifteenth?"

"Sure."

"Wasn't fifteenth two nights ago?"

"Wasn't? No, wasn't. First time I ever know him to come any time other than first an' fifteenth."

"Good."

"Bully," she said. She looked at me. "Who'n hell you think you are? Fancy pants?"

"Disguise. I'm a private *ojo*."

"Oho!" she said. "What's oho?"

"Spanish for eye. I'm a private eye. Like in eyeball."

She shuddered. "Ugh," she said. "Don't ever say that word again. Shell. Hey, Shell."

"Yeah?"

"'Nother drink?"

"Sure. Sure." I made it over to the dresser, mixed the drinks, and came back to the beds. She sure looked good on those beds.

She said, "Toast. Toast somebody."

"Toast Eisenhower. Good ol' boy, he."

"Good. Bully for Eisenheimer."

"Howmer. Eisenhowmer, stupid."

We toasted Owmenheiser.

She got up, poured more drinks, and came back. "Li'l toast," she said. She looked toward me. "Toast Bernard Brooch," she said.

We drank the toast.

She fixed two more. She handed me a glass and we clinked the glasses together.

"Toas'," she said. "Bully ol' toas'. Toas' Truman. Give ol' Harry a toas'."

"*Lorraine!*" I said. "You're getting *drunk!*"

There was a moment of silence. She blinked at me.

"Guess I am," she said. "You're drunk, too. Bet you're always drunk. Shell's jus' an ol' drunk drunk."

"That's unkind, Lorraine. Not nice. Just because I'm a little tiny bit woozy. No, sir, ma'am. You're striking below the belt."

She leaned close to me. "Shell," she whispered slowly, "don' you remember? I'm striking all over."

"Shh," I said. "Never did tell you how much I enjoyed your dance at Pelican. Tell you now. Really 'joyed it."

She smiled happily. "Thank you, thank you. I'll dance for you, jus' for you. You wanna dance with me?"

"Wanna dance with you? Do I wanna dance with you? Just you ask me."

She was up off the bed now, moving around the room, moving every which way and humming and singing trala-la and bum-diddy-bum, and if she'd looked carefully at me right then she might have thought I still had on my fake eyeballs. I rose and walked to her and grabbed her.

"This kills me," I said. "I'm getting old."

"Not old. Nice."

"Old. Old, old man. I can feel my arteries hardening. I creak when I walk. C'mere."

"No, no, no," she said. "You wait. Gonna dance."

I waited, and I'm glad I waited. She backed across the room and it was just as it had been on that first night when I'd seen her dance at the Pelican: I forgot about everything except the wild, wild woman. She moved easily and gracefully at first, smiling all the time and humming her own music as she fumbled with the blouse and pulled it from her smooth shoulders. Then she reached behind her to unfasten her brassiere, shrugged it from her arms, and dropped it to the floor, looking squarely at me and chuckling softly. I could feel my face getting hot. This was another fire dance, a private one, and I felt as if I were the fuel. Lorraine stood with her hands on her hips, her shoulders thrown back and her heavy breasts thrusting forward, pink-tipped and erect and swaying slightly as she paused for only a moment and then stepped toward me. It was surprising how much better they looked without any gold dust.

I was paralyzed. Well, practically paralyzed: I couldn't move my feet. She backed away from me, fingering the zipper at the side of her brown skirt. I was breathing through my mouth and my throat was dry as I heard the faint hiss of the pulled zipper and the rustle of cloth as the skirt fell to Lorraine's feet. She took one step toward me and out of a pink silk wisp, then stood motionless in the bright glow of the overhead lights, naked except for her high-heeled shoes and rolled nylons.

I stared at her as she laughed softly, then went into the dance she'd promised me: the frantic, twisting body, thrusting spasmodically, writhing and turning, everything the same as it had been at the Pelican. Maybe it was the only routine she knew, but when you came right down to it, it was the only one she would ever need. It was the only one any woman would ever need.

After what might have been minutes, she walked across the room toward me and stopped, smiling up at me, with the erect tips of her breasts brushing the front of my shirt. I put my arms around her, the skin of her back warm against the moist palms of my hands, and she melted against me as I kissed her on her pouting lips, her cheek, her throat. Neither of us remembered to turn off the lights. . .

Later Lorraine took our glasses to the dresser and mixed two more drinks, still laughing at something I'd said. I tried to think of something else funny. She certainly looked terrific laughing like that. I went over to the dresser and stood behind her.

"Go 'way," she said.

95

"Uh-uh. I'm not thirsty." I put a hand on her arm and turned her around. She wiggled away from me, laughing merrily. I guess it was away from me. Lorraine looked wonderful when I could focus on her.

"Hold still," I said. "I wanna focus on you."

She squealed and struggled weakly. "You relax," she said. "I hate you."

I got a good hold on her and backed her up into a corner and I kissed her with feeling. She didn't mind the kiss, but she objected to the feeling. At least, she said she objected, but I was pretty sure she was kidding—and she smiled when she said that.

"Shell," she laughed, "I didn't know you felt that way."

I said, "C'mere."

She scooted toward the bed, but I grabbed her. She looked up at me. "Watch this," she said, and shoved away from me. She broke into a cute little step and I broke into a cold sweat. Then she was up close to me again, and I was up close to her again, and we went waltzing around the room.

She was light on her feet, all right; her feet seemed hardly to touch the floor, she was so light on her feet. There wasn't any music but it didn't seem to bother her. Didn't seem to bother me. And she was such a good dancer that she could probably have followed anybody, but, man, we danced well together.

16

I WOKE UP and my room looked funny and my head felt horrible. I opened my eyes like a man making two slow incisions and squinted at this funny room. I got out of bed and hobbled toward the dresser and a woman came out of the next room.

I looked at her. She was wearing a quilted bathrobe and was holding something on her head with her right hand. She was holding an ice bag on her head.

I said, "What the hell are you doing in my room?"

She groaned at me.

I looked into the mirror. A strange man with black eyebrows and red eyes peered out at me. Hell, I wasn't even in my room. And then it occurred to me that this fellow in the mirror was me, and that this was Lorraine's room, and everything came back to me like crazy.

I jumped to the bed and pulled a blanket around me.

"Coy," Lorraine said. "He's coy."

"My God," I said. "What time is it?"

"Time for you to get out of my life. Forever. You've killed me. Oh, my head. I think it's ruined. Look at my head, Shell. Is it split?"

97

The shape I was in, I actually went over and looked at it. "No," I said soberly. "It's all right. Nothing wrong with it."

She glared at me. "A fat lot you know," she said. "It's *my* head."

She took her head back into the next room, and I got dressed in my Mexican costume, complete with gun. The way my hand was wobbling, if I'd tried to shoot anyone then I'd probably have blown my brains out. I went to the door of the next room and knocked.

Lorraine opened the door.

"I'm leaving," I said.

"I'm sick," she said. "Sicker than a dog. Much sicker. Dogs got no troubles at all."

"Lorraine, I'm leaving."

"Boy, am I sick."

"Lorraine. Good-by, Lorraine. I'll call you."

"Don't you dare."

"Uh, don't mention to Dante that I was here."

"Are you mad, Dad? I won't mention it to anybody."

I nodded, then put a hand to my throbbing head. "Well, good-by." I went to the front door. Behind me Lorraine said something unintelligible and shut her door again.

I looked at my watch. It was already nearly one in the afternoon. I hunched over, kept my face under the brim of the sombrero, and found the stairs leading down. I kept my face turned toward the floor and brushed past stupid people who were actually laughing. But I made it outside into the bright and painful sunlight. A little bird screamed at me.

A half block away was a bar called Chloe's, the closest place to Dante's Inferno. I headed toward it, hoping that I didn't run into Dante or any of his friends, because they'd have little trouble with me right at this moment.

I put a call through to the Desert Inn and gave the number of Colleen's room. While the phone buzzed I felt the tenseness growing in me, and I remembered how innocent and at the same time sensual Colleen had looked when I'd first seen her sitting at the Lady Luck Bar. And for the first time in a long, long time I felt a little remorse for the night I'd just passed. Not that I was thinking about Lorraine, but that I was remembering Colleen and her wide-eyed, smiling face, and the full woman's curves of her magnificent body.

And then that crackly voice said in my ear, "Hello. . . hello."

"Colleen? Colleen, is that you? Are you all right?"

"Shell?"

"Yeah, honey. Are you O.K.?"

"Oh, yes. Where are you, Shell? What happened to you?"

"I'm at Chloe's. I was just going to ask you where you disappeared to."

98

"Are you all right?"

"I'm alive. Where you been?"

"Right here. In my room. I kept calling your room and calling it, but there wasn't any answer. I was afraid. . . "

"Honey, I couldn't go back to my room. That's where those three goons picked me up. I'll explain about it. And I'll never be able to thank you enough for getting me out of that mess last night, Colleen. They really would have killed me if it hadn't been for you."

"Never mind that now, Shell. Want me to pick you up?"

"Well—it might not be a good idea for you to wander around. After last night, maybe—"

"Oh, nonsense. Nobody knows I had anything to do with you—or with that. Those two men with me were too drunk to remember, and I had breakfast in the Cactus Room this morning and nobody even noticed me. That's where I. . . got the knife. So I'll be right down. You be out in front of Chloe's in two minutes." She hung up.

I walked out in front of the club and waited. In about two minutes I saw Colleen's Mercury wheel in at the drive and pull up in front of the club. She went right past me, stopped the car, and started looking around, a worried look on her face.

I'd forgotten about my damned outfit. I said, "Hey, here I am. I'm uh, disguised."

I walked up to the car and she got one good look at me and almost busted laughing. I climbed in beside her and she took my hand and squeezed it. I explained briefly why I was in the flashy getup. She kept laughing and finally she said, "I don't know whether it's because I'm so glad to see you, or because you look so silly. But I couldn't help laughing."

"I am kind of a mess, I suppose."

"You are." She put the car in gear and asked me, "Where to?"

"Down to Fremont. My clothes are there."

She shook her head, but drove downtown. When we got to the store she wouldn't let me go in, "They'd throw you in jail," she said. She came back with the box of my clothes and we headed back to Fifth and out toward the Strip again.

Then she asked, "Where now?"

"Damned if I know, Colleen. I've got to get some food and think a few things out."

She said, "If you can't go back to your own room, you can use mine. Where did you spend the night?"

That was a nice one to throw at me. I could either tell her the truth or lie to her, and somehow I didn't feel like lying to Colleen. So I told her. "I went to a spot on the Strip last night to talk to a woman. She had information about the case I'm on, information that I needed. That's the truth about why I went to see her. She had a room in the hotel and I stayed there."

She didn't say anything for several seconds, then she said, "Thanks for telling me. You didn't have to. But I wish you'd called me."

"I did. I called you half a dozen times before I left the Desert Inn, but there wasn't any answer. After that I—I got drunk. I got drunk and went to sleep."

Finally she looked at me and smiled slightly. "Well, you can still use my room. For your food and thinking."

We were at the Desert Inn by now. I said, "You'd better go on in by yourself, Colleen. I'll follow you in a few minutes. No sense our walking around together in broad daylight."

"You don't want to be seen with me?" She was smiling.

"Just the opposite. I don't want you seen with me. Not, at least, while I'm so unpopular. Go on."

She parked over at the left of the main entrance, got out, and went inside. I waited three or four minutes, then went inside all stooped over, a very simple position for me to assume right then. Nobody bothered me and I got to Colleen's room without any trouble. Probably a few sympathetic people looked at the poor, sick old caballero creeping across the lobby, but that was all. I knocked and Colleen let me in, then locked the door.

I made it to a big easy chair, turned around, and sank down into it as Colleen walked across the room toward me. Even as beat-up as I was, I couldn't keep my eyes off those trim, shapely legs. Then Colleen was leaning forward over my chair, one hand on each chair arm, and I found it difficult to believe that a woman could have two such beautiful legs without their being her outstanding characteristics. But they weren't, because there, looking right back at me, were the two that were.

She was wearing brown pumps and sheer nylons, a tan skirt, and a light green blouse with a wide collar and only the top two buttons unbuttoned. The top two were enough, and almost one too many. I noticed again the rust-red hair piled high on top of her head—and I like a woman to have luxuriant hair; that is, I'm of the apparently outmoded school that believes a woman should look like a woman and not come out of a beauty shop looking as if she'd just had a man's haircut and, possibly, a shave.

She was still leaning forward, looking at me, and she said with a slight smile, "You look as if you need some more rest, Shell. Want to nap a while?"

I shook my head. Slowly. "I don't need any more sleep. Coffee and a few hours of breathing should fix me up."

"Want a big breakfast?"

"Not yet."

She went to the phone, ordered orange juice, toast, and a pot of coffee, then sat down in another chair near me.

I said, "Let me tell you now, Colleen. I'm in your debt for last night. You really did save my life. Sure as fate those guys would have killed me, and I want—"

She stopped me. "That's enough, Shell. I didn't even think about it when it happened. I was already wondering why you were so late coming to the bar." She smiled. "It's supposed to be the woman who's always late."

I grinned at her. "Thank God you're a punctual woman. Want to bring me up to date on you?"

She told me she'd run and grabbed the knife, then picked up the two drunks and gone out the side entrance. After giving me the knife, she'd run to her car. "I was scared to death," she said. "It was pretty dark then and I don't know what happened. I must have sat there for half an hour or more. Police cars came up and some men were out there where you were. I didn't even know it wasn't you, Shell."

"It was a couple of those friends of mine. The third one beat it."

"Oh. Then I drove around for a while. I guess I was partly looking to see if you were around anywhere, and partly just driving and calming down."

I told her briefly what had happened to me. While I was talking the food came and I kept out of sight while she took the tray. I had the juice and toast while I finished, then started on the black coffee.

"What are you going to do now?" she asked me.

I shook my head. "I don't know, Colleen. I've got a lot of odds and ends, but I don't know where all of them fit. I'm pretty damn confused." I looked over at her. "*Your* maiden name wouldn't have been Isabel Bing, would it?"

She laughed. "No, sir. Isabel Bing. What a name! Isn't that a horrible name, Shell? No, I was Colleen Shawn, just as I am now. When I got my divorce I asked for my maiden name back. From Mrs. Colleen Raymond back to Colleen Shawn."

She didn't want any coffee, so I poured another cup for myself and said, "Colleen Shawn. *That's* a lovely name, and for a lovely woman. I think something like that was the first thing I said to you, wasn't it?"

She laughed. "Nope. You said, 'Hello, you're wonderful.' I remember. And you'd never even seen me before."

"Didn't have to. And I still don't know much about you. What are some of the details?"

She leaned back in her chair and crossed her legs. "What do you want to know?"

"Everything."

"You said that before, too. Well, I'm twenty-five. I'm from back East, Connecticut. Born there. Went to school in Connecticut with little-girl ambitions to be a fashion designer. My folks died when I was in college and I came out here to the West Coast and worked in clothing stores up in San Francisco till I met Bob—Robert Raymond, that is. I guess I was tired of working every day, and being lonely a lot of the time. Anyway, we got married. It lasted eleven months, and it just wasn't right. So we reached an amicable parting and I came here to Las Vegas. That was a couple of months ago. I established the six weeks' residence required here for divorce, and now I'm Colleen Shawn again. Since I got my name back I've been relaxing here, because it's a nice place to relax."

I grinned at her. "Not lately it isn't."

She looked at me. "You certainly look silly," she said.

I'd forgotten my costume again. I said, "Time I did something about that. Mind if I change here?"

"Use the bathroom. And use the shower, too, if you want. Get rid of those black eyebrows—I like them better the other way."

I finished my coffee, got up, and took my gabardine suit out of the box. I took everything out of the pockets and put it on the dresser. "Do you mind if I clutter the place up temporarily?" I asked Colleen.

"Go ahead. I'm used to masculine clutter, you know."

I piled the stuff on the dresser. Last night I'd left everything except my wallet in my suit when I left the costume shop. That had sure been potent bourbon. Anyway, now I wanted to be sure my stuff was all here. In a little row, I strung out my wallet, J. Harrison Bing's card, a set of keys to my L.A. rooms and office—a separate set from the keys to the bombed Cadillac; the police still had those—the key to my room here at the Desert Inn, which I'd never turned in at the desk, change, handkerchief, and comb. Something about the collection stirred a bit in my mind but settled down and I went into the bathroom.

I hung up the clothes, undressed, and climbed into the shower, as hot as I could stand it. While I soaped up and groaned and scrubbed my hair and eyebrows I thought of the things that had happened so far on the case. Even though I'd been running around like a scared rabbit and most of the time been running from or into trouble, I'd managed to pick up quite a pile of information in the less than three days I'd been on the case. And I had the funny feeling I sometimes get on a job, the subconscious stirring as if to say the answer's down in there, all ready to be plucked out. It made my skin tingle a little, but I couldn't pin down what it was. I didn't push it.

Colleen yelled from the other room, "Shell, don't you sing in the shower?"

"Once in a while. Not this time, though. Want to harmonize a little?"

I heard her laugh, but she didn't answer. I rinsed soap off me, then scrubbed my hair some more while I thought about Colleen. Something she'd mentioned a few minutes ago had started me thinking, too. Little bits of information and conversation were ganging up in my brain.

I rinsed off, got out of the shower, and toweled down, then got into my clothes and went into the other room.

Colleen said, "Hi. Feel better?"

"Like a new man. Pretty soon I'll chew a steak and I'll be ready to take off."

"For where?" She tucked her skirt under her and swung her legs over the arm of the chair she was sitting in.

"Tell you the truth, I'm not sure yet. I've got to think it out a little more."

She looked down at my feet. "Barefoot boy. I'll bet you were always stubbing your toes when you were a kid."

"You're right. And stepping on pieces of glass and nails."

"Farm boy?"

"City boy. Los Angeles. Born and raised there. Lived there all my life except when I was knocking around the country or learning the most effective ways to kill other people in wars."

She was quiet for a while, then she said, "Los Angeles. I've never been there. I'd like to see your City of Angels."

"A misnomer," I said. "Ain't no angels. But I'd love to show you the town. I know almost every inch of the place, and I've got some friends in Hollywood if you should want to hit the studios."

She smiled. "You've got yourself a date, Mr. Scott. Are you going straight back to L.A. when you're through up here?"

"I'd like to. If this winds up O.K."

"If?"

"When, I mean. But, frankly, I may be in jail."

She looked puzzled, and I explained. "I may not have made it clear, Colleen, but one of the reasons I don't want to go back to my room—besides keeping away from some bruisers—is that I don't care to talk to the sheriff right now. Last night when I got away from those three musclemen, I killed one of them."

She swallowed and her eyes got wider, but she didn't say anything. I went on, "Maybe two of them."

"What'll they do, Shell? To you, I mean."

"Depends on a lot of things, including how the D. A. feels. He's the man who has to be satisfied. But the guy had a gun and was going to use it when I hit him."

"Hit him? With your hand?"

"Uh-huh. The other one got the knife, but the one I know is dead got the edge of my hand."

She frowned, staring at me. "I don't understand. You just hit him and it killed him?"

"That's one of the things I mentioned a few minutes ago, honey. About learning how to kill people when I went not so gaily off to war. There are a surprising number of ways to kill people with your bare hands, and in only part of a second. That's one of the things the services, especially the Marines, teach men—mainly so they can stay alive. But when you've taught a man how to kill quickly and efficiently so he can go fight your wars for you, you've done something you can't take back. That knowledge is in his brain and you can't wipe it out or pretend it isn't there simply by ignoring it. And if the man is well trained, like almost all Marines are, then a lot of that training becomes damn near a reflex action, automatic. I. . . probably didn't have to kill that man last night. If I hadn't, he might have killed me, but part of it was reflex, pure and simple. There was a man there, he intended to kill me, and I reacted the way I was trained a good many years ago to react. It's as simple as that. If I live to be a hundred, there'll still be part of that left in me."

I stopped and then added, "I'm sorry, Colleen. I didn't mean to make a speech." I grinned at her. "Besides, it isn't likely I'll live to be a hundred."

After a few moments she said, "I didn't mind the speech. You did get a bit wound up, though. You should have seen your face."

I laughed. "That's one of my great good fortunes. I don't have to see my face."

"Oh, I don't know," she said. "It's not such a bad face. Well, now I'm going to take a shower. You stretch out on the bed and relax." She smiled. "You're not so hardboiled as you sound."

"I feel very soft-boiled at the moment. Get on with you now, my Irish Colleen. Go shower that incredible body of yours." She paused in the doorway and looked back at me and I said, "You are a damned beautiful woman."

"Sure now," she said smiling, "next you'll be telling me I'm your own true darlin'."

I grinned at her. "I'll be telling you more than that."

She smiled at me for a long second, and there was a hint of the transformation I'd seen come over that innocent face once before, at the bar when she'd pressed her hand against my lips. Then she turned and shut the door behind her.

I was wondering if she'd locked the door, and if she had, if I were strong enough yet to break the door down, but then I sighed and got up and went over to the bed. I stretched out on it, relaxed, and ran over again in my mind the things that had happened so far in this case, from the very beginning till now. There were several screwy angles, but I knew one thing: If Isabel were really still alive, I'd like to meet her face to face, know that it *was* Isabel, and ask her some pertinent questions.

Something flickered in my mind, then faded away before I could grab it and pin it down. I felt the excitement tingle in me, but I lay quietly listening to the drumming of the shower in the next room, and tried to get that thought back again. I tried to think what it was, shook my head, and right then, just as if the shaking of my head had tumbled the final part into place, I got it.

I got just a piece of it, and then all the rest of the pieces leaped up in my mind as if they had been waiting for the one thought that would release them and let them spring into place. I knew right then, with a kind of breathless excitement inside me, that this crazy case was solved, that I knew the answers now, knew where Isabel was and why Carter was killed and why Freddy was killed and all the rest, and I also knew I was going to have to visit Mrs. Victor Dante's bedroom.

17

I LET OUT a whoop and the shower stopped drumming on that lovely stuff it was drumming on in there. There was a moment of silence.

Then Colleen called, "Was that you, Shell?"

"That was me, Shell Scott, the one and only scintillating shamus."

"What's the matter? You all right?"

"I'm fine; I'm dandy. Come on out and I'll dry your back."

"Oh, Shell!"

"Think I'm kidding?"

The shower started drumming again.

I stretched out on the bed, feeling pretty good. I knew my next move was to go out to Dante's place. But not right now. I wanted darkness around me when I started in again; I also wanted my strength back. I wanted a steak or some prime ribs inside me, I wanted a drink, and I wanted to rest up some more and think the whole business through.

The bathroom door opened and Colleen came out into the room. She had one of those huge, fuzzy towels wrapped around her body, covering her breasts and extending halfway down her thighs, but that was all she had on.

I made a sort of strangled noise and started to get up, but she stopped in the middle of the room and, holding the towel up with her right hand, she pointed her left hand at me.

"You stay right where you are, Mr. Scott," she said, smiling. "I've got to get some clothes on."

"What for?" I croaked. "Let's not be hasty. Schiaparelli never designed a more fetching gown."

"Sit down, Mr. Scott."

"Shell. But—"

"No buts." She meant it. No buts.

I opened my mouth and she said, "You might as well relax." She held the towel with her right hand, the other hand on her hip, and she said with her lips twisted slightly in a soft smile, "I'm not kidding. If you think you can roam all over town all night, and wind up in strange ladies' hotel rooms, then come up here and do as you please—"

"She wasn't a strange lady, I mean, I wasn't roaming all. . . I mean, well, you know, I mean. . . "

She stood there with that damned little smile on her face till I petered out. Then she went to the closet and selected some clothes, went to the dresser and pulled out some delightfully frilly little things that were black and gossamer, and undulated back into the bathroom. She closed the door firmly.

I sure shouldn't have told her a thing.

She came out fully dressed in a black skirt and a pink sweater, and I'd never seen her in a sweater before, but right away I knew I should have. I also knew that everything in that sweater was Colleen and not stamped with a union label. When they started stamping *those* with labels, then I was joining the union, and I'd fight like hell for a closed shop. She had on nylon hose and high-heeled shoes, and her hair was still high on her head. She was all dressed up from tip to toe.

I looked at her as she sat down in the easy chair again. "I feel all naked," I said. "Where the hell are my goddamn shoes?"

She laughed with that delightful crackle in her voice and she said, "They're right there in the bathroom. You'd better put them on. People might talk."

"Then they'd certainly be talking through their ears," I said.

"Hungry yet?"

"I'm ravenous."

"Are you *hungry*?"

I grinned at her. "Yeah. Order me a steak and a knife and fork. I gotta have something to keep my hands occupied."

She ordered the food from room service while I put on my lousy shoes. But even so, the rest of that afternoon was one of the pleasantest I can remember.

107

Colleen was sure as hell sticking to her determination that I was to keep my distance, but we had two meals together and a lot of conversation. All afternoon, as it got closer to dusk, I kept thinking that this was really a woman, this Colleen Shawn. She was beautiful, she was sexy as a handpicked harem, and in addition to that she was fun, just plain fun to talk to. She was interesting, too, and she made me laugh, and then laughed at me or with me. There are damned few women you can spend an afternoon with in a hotel room, alone, just talking, and still have a hell of a good time. But this Colleen of mine certainly was one.

Finally the shadows were lengthening outside and the mountains were getting purple, and it was almost time for me to go. We'd sent for a bottle earlier and had a couple of highballs together after a delicious prime-rib dinner in her room, and I got up and mixed two more drinks.

"Colleen," I said, "after this one I have to go. But this one's for you, because you're a wonderful woman. And I mean it."

She took the glass I handed her and said, "Thank you, Shell." We sipped our drinks while it got darker outside.

She said, "I meant it about seeing Los Angeles with you. Still want to take me out in your town?"

"I'd like nothing better. We'll hit Mocambo, Ciro's, some of the little spots around L.A. and Hollywood too."

"You can lead the way."

I got up and walked over to the phone. It took only five minutes and two calls, and when I was through I had the address of Victor Dante's home, and a taxi on its way to the Desert Inn for me. Colleen stood next to me and listened while I phoned.

I hadn't been wearing my gun or holster while Colleen and I sat alone in the room, but now that I was ready to leave I got the gun, strapped it on, and put on my tie and then my coat.

Colleen said, "You're going to Dante's?"

"Uh-huh. I'll see you later, honey."

"Shell, will you be all right? I mean, you won't get hurt?"

"I'll be all right."

"Please don't lie to me, Shell. Is there any chance you'll be hurt?"

"Oh, hell, there's always a chance, Colleen. I might trip on a rug and break my fool neck. But what I've got to do shouldn't get me in any trouble. I'll be back before you miss me. Honestly."

I went to the door and turned the knob.

"It's still locked," Colleen said. "Just a minute."

She got up and went to the dresser, got the key, and came over by me. She unlocked the door and I reached for the knob.

108

"So long, honey," I said.

"Shell." Her voice was tight, but soft, and she was close to me.

I turned, with my back to the door, and looked down at her upturned face and at the narrowed brown eyes. Her lips were parted and moist, and she took both my wrists in her hands and put them around her waist. She pressed herself against me and said, "Kiss me. Shell, kiss me."

I started to speak, but I only started to, because I was talking between her warm lips and looking at her long lashes trembling over her closed eyes, and then my eyes were closed and her tongue stopped any more words from coming.

I kissed her till her mouth and my mouth seemed like flesh fused together and she was pressed hard against me. We were thigh to thigh, stomach to stomach, her breasts mashed against my chest, and our arms around each other straining our bodies together. And she was liquid, like water or quicksilver, moving, never still, her body as fluid and demanding as her darting tongue in my mouth.

Finally she broke away, pushed her hands against my chest, and held me from her like that, her breasts rising and falling with her rapid breathing. I started to speak but she pressed her fingers to my lips and said, "No, go on, Shell. But come back to me."

Then she opened the door, and I went out of her room, out of the Desert Inn, and got into the taxi waiting to take me to Victor Dante's home.

18

DANTE'S home was out in the desert four or five miles farther out than the end of the Strip and a half mile or so off Highway 91, and as the taxi got nearer I tried to calm myself and collect my thoughts. I had trouble because I was still thinking about Colleen, but it was time I started concentrating on the work ahead. If it could be called work. If I had to, I was going to bust in Mrs. Dante's bedroom, but I hoped that wouldn't be necessary because all I wanted to do was get positive identification of the little blonde gal who'd plopped off the stool at the Lady Luck Bar. And remembering that I knew only one mark, a scar, that would identify the missing Isabel, I shook my head and clucked my tongue. Because voyeurism was rampant in the desert tonight, and in the interest of justice I was about to become, let's face it, a peeper. Scott, you devil, you.

I got out of the taxi just off Highway 91, paid the driver, and watched him drive away. Then I turned around and started walking the half mile to my destination. I was there in less than ten minutes. It was a big, new, modernistic place, low to the ground and built with lots of glass to let in the desert sun. There were lights on inside, so I knew somebody was home, but that was the way I had it figured. Logically Dante would be at the Inferno, and the little lovely who'd had such an entrancing walk before she'd fainted wouldn't be likely to be running around town for a while after that. So the gal with Hogarth's lovely curve should be inside there.

Ten minutes later I'd found what I assumed was the bedroom, or at least one of them, but I couldn't be sure, even though the window was wide open, because no light was on inside. But I picked my spot, then walked quietly around to the front again to look into the living room, where lights were burning. I took out my gun and held it ready in my hand just in case.

There was a wide porch in front of the house and I walked gently across it to the window and found a spot where I could look through. There was a thin curtain behind the window, and I had to look through that, but she was in there, all right.

It was the little blonde gal with the feather cut that the bartender had pointed out as Mrs. Dante. She was sitting in a low, modernistic chair with her profile toward me, reading a book. She wasn't dressed in the tailored slacks and black sweater she'd been wearing when she caught my eye at the Desert Inn dice table, but she had on a heavy silk dressing gown and fluffy slippers. I made sure it was the same gal, then walked about fifty feet away from the house and waited.

I felt a little nervous waiting out there in the desert sitting with sagebrush at my back. It wasn't that I was afraid anybody would start shooting at me, but rather that this was hardly my usual method of investigation. This afternoon, when there'd been that little activity in my brain cells, it had become necessary that I find out if little Blondie was the gal who'd exploded firecrackers under tin cans, and find out for sure. Preferably in a hurry. If I were wrong, that hadn't been logical thinking this afternoon, but a brain fit, and I was right back to where I'd started.

About an hour after I started my wait, the lights went out in the front room and I got to my feet. I started wishing I had the rest of that bottle I'd left with Colleen, because I sure could have used a drink. But I walked around in back of the house and the light was on in what I'd assumed was the bedroom. This was the only house for miles, a hundred yards from the narrow dirt road that led here from the main highway, and Blondie must by now have felt completely safe from prying eyes. Faint light spilled from the open window and fell dimly on the ground outside, and from where I was, thirty or forty feet from the house, I saw her walk across the room.

I hoped this peeping act of mine wasn't a waste of time, because I wanted to wind this caper up tonight if I could. I was damn tired of hiding from gunmen. I walked clear up to the window and stood just out of the dim splash of light coming from a lamp over the bed, just as she crossed the room from my

111

right to my left and went through a door in the left wall and swung the door nearly shut behind her.

The stupid woman still had on that damn robe. No cooperation. I moved close to the window and watched the door in the far wall. I might get only one chance, if that, and I didn't want to miss it. I could hear her humming as if she were happy. I wasn't happy. I was damn near hysterical. I was in a cold sweat.

Then she came through the door and I was in a hot sweat. She didn't have a stitch on except for a wide ribbon that held her hair back from her face. During a moment when my gaze wandered I saw that her face was covered with a thin film of some sort of pink cream.

The head of the low Hollywood bed was across the room opposite me, the foot of the bed extending back toward me, and she walked across the room and stood at the left side of the bed opposite me, facing me.

Damn. That was the wrong way for her to face. The hell it was the wrong way for her to face. But it was the wrong way for the success of my investigation. I was certainly uncomfortable. But I didn't know whether it was because I was afraid she'd turn out the light before I'd got what I'd come out here for, or because I was afraid somebody would see me and start false rumors about me. False rumors, hell, they'd be true. And already I was within an inch of changing my mind about what I *had* come out here for.

She stood facing me squarely and put both hands high over her head. Near fainting, I thought, My God! Does she know I'm out here?

But then I remembered that I'd thought she must play a lot of tennis or do a lot of exercises or visit masseurs regularly to keep that trim, compact body in such excellent shape; now I knew it wasn't tennis or masseurs. She was exercising. You know: stretch, bend, and touch the toes; stretch, bend, and so on. This gal was in earnest, just as if she were keeping time to music. One, two, three, four. One, two, three, four. A snatch of an old burlesque tune flashed through my mind. And then another. As a matter of fact, several snatches flashed through my mind.

I was bending at the knees and swaying when she finished, and then she scooted over on the bed. I thought for one horrible moment that she was going to turn out the bed lamp, turn over, and go to sleep, and that all of this time would have been, ha-ha, wasted. But this gal wasn't through.

There is an exercise that is excellent for toning one's stomach muscles. One lies on one's back on the floor or the bed, and one slowly lifts one's lower limbs high into the air and, with the toes, touches the floor or bed above one's head. This is *excellent* for strengthening the abdominal musculature and is highly recommended by health experts and, from this day forward, by me. But, usually, if you're not used to so strenuous an exercise, about ten of those things will ruin you for days. Ruined me for days.

112

And the little peroxide blonde was still working on the problem of keeping herself in shape, which is like trying to knock home runs one foot higher over the fence, but she slowly started to tone her stomach muscles.

I was swaying back and forth, and I damn near lost my balance and fell into the room. But now I knew that my sleuthing was going to pay off: In just a second I'd know the truth about Mrs. Dante.

It was there! And right where I thought it would be. The scar was a thin white line about four inches long and slanting back at the end like half an arrowhead, and even though it was difficult to see through the water in my eyes, I made it out. There was no doubt about it: Right there was where the can had hit her.

And that took care of that. I felt a little silly standing outside a window like a Peeping Tom and staring at a naked woman doing her exercises. So I left.

I turned around and started walking back into the desert, but I couldn't help thinking that she must have been doing those exercises for a long time. Because you know what? She did twenty of those things.

A half hour later I dug my client's card out of my wallet. I squinted carefully at it in the light of a phone booth, then I called J. Harrison Bing and in a fast three-minute conversation told him to get up to Las Vegas fast because his daughter was here and was sure as hell going to be in trouble before morning and need some moral support. He squawked and sputtered, but I drove my point home and finally he said he'd be up on the very next plane. I gave him the address of the desert house and told him I'd meet him there.

Then I hung up, feeling very damned proud of myself, and went to the Inferno and killed Victor Dante.

19

I T WASN'T that I went to the Inferno to kill the man; that was the last thing I wanted to do. All I wanted to do was get Dante and turn him over to the county sheriff. I had my reasons for charging around like a one-man army instead of gathering a crew of armed police and deputies about me, too. Law-enforcement agencies never look with a happy eye upon somebody who has killed another man, as I had, and I was in deep enough now so that I wanted all the weight of evidence—and all the friendly feelings I could get—on my side before I went to the courthouse and started explaining. I wanted to lay the whole mess in their laps, tied up with a pink ribbon, before I took a chance on getting tossed in the cooler and having this case blow up in my face. And it could still blow up, even though I thought I had almost all of it now, except for some little things. Things I might get from Dante.

And, of course, there was the personal angle, too. Dante had been growing on me like a boil for almost seventy-two hours, and this thing between him and me had now come to a very personal head. But I wanted him alive and talking; he had to get smart. No pink ribbon for me.

I'd called Bing from a service station I'd walked to at ten-forty-five P.M. It took me another half hour to get a cab and ride downtown to Fremont

Street. In one of the clothing stores there I bought my third cowboy hat of this Helldorado. Then I phoned the Inferno, pretending to be a drunk trying to make reservations for the floor show at El Rancho Vegas, and found out that Dante was in his office. While I was in the booth I called the airport and learned that the next plane was already on its way and would land at Las Vegas at one-ten A.M. It was eleven-thirty now, so that meant I had over an hour and a half before Bing arrived. I figured that was plenty of time, so I crammed my Stetson on my head, caught a cab, and was on my way to see Victor Dante.

Getting to his office was the easiest part. I got out of the cab at the main entrance to the Inferno, and walked right in behind a party of four enjoying this third night of Helldorado. I kept my head down, walked straight across the lobby, into the Devil's Room, and along the length of the bar with my gun in my coat pocket and my right hand on my gun. It took less than half a minute, and Dante and his men couldn't be expected to have their eyes peeled for me sixty minutes an hour, twenty-four hours a day. I walked right into the empty hallway, across it, and up to Dante's door.

I was trying to make myself relax, keep as calm as possible now that I was so close, but my heart was pounding and my throat was tight as I squeezed the doorknob in my left hand and turned it gently as I lifted the gun from my pocket with my right. The door was locked.

There's no good reason for a man in a night club to keep his door locked, because polite people usually knock anyway, but the damn thing was locked. I eased my hand off the knob and looked up and down the hallway while I waited to find out if anybody inside the office had noticed the knob turning, and it occurred to me that this would be one lousy time for somebody to spot me while I stood in front of Dante's door with a gun in my hand.

Nobody was yet in the hallway, but I could hear the steady rumble of voices from the crowd in the game room at my back, behind the wall, and occasionally the louder drone of the dealers. Ten seconds passed and nothing happened, but I could hear somebody moving around inside the office. Well, if I had to knock, this was no time to be timid about it. I raised my left hand and slammed my knuckles hard into the wooden panel half a dozen times. Then, as footsteps came closer to me on the other side of the panel, I stuck the two-inch barrel of my .38 up at the crack of the door and waited.

The steps came clear up to the door and stopped, and I knew he was only a foot away from me now, separated from me by only a half inch of wood. Then I heard a bolt slide back inside. The door started to open and I slammed into it and stuck my gun right up against Dante's still bruised and puffy mouth. He stumbled backwards as the swinging door hit him, and I stepped inside and gave the office a fast look to make sure we had the place to our-

115

selves. We did. It was just Victor Dante and me now, and he wasn't near any buzzers, or even near his big desk.

He'd stumbled away from me, but he caught his balance and stared at me from his small eyes, with his mouth open slightly, as I caught the door and slammed it shut.

"Don't even move, Dante," I said quietly. "Don't buzz for anybody, don't yell, don't even make a noise. Just stand right there."

He stood there, and he didn't jump me—not with my gun pointed at him from six feet away—but he did make a little noise. He said, "You damned fool. You are a fool, Scott. This time you're finished."

His voice was flat and brittle, but the words were distorted a little as they passed his split lips. He was dying to get at me; it stood out all over him. It showed in his cold eyes and all over his hard, frozen face, even in the way he stood looking at me with his fists clenched and his head stuck forward toward me.

I said, "I was finished last time, too. But you're the one that's through, Dante. Get this: I know it all. I know the whole damned thing. I know about Carter and Freddy and all the rest of it. And I'm handing you over to the sheriff and I'll be their fair-haired boy. You should have killed Lorraine, too, friend. Or was that next?"

He didn't answer for a moment. Then he said, "You can't possibly think you'll get out of here again."

"I'm not even going to try," I told him. "I don't have to." I nodded toward his desk. "You've got a phone there. All I have to do is use it. After I work you over a little."

He glanced toward the phone, and for the first time that frozen face cracked a little bit. He looked back at me and licked his lips, then winced and put a hand to his mouth. His eyes flicked around the room, but there wasn't anything in sight that would help him.

"The sheriff wouldn't know what to do with me," he said after a pause. "You're out of your mind."

"He'll know what to do after I talk to him for half an hour. I'll turn you over to him, Dante, then we'll run out to see your peroxide mistress."

"My what?" He looked surprised.

I didn't say anything.

He said, "You can't mean Crystal. She's my wife."

I grinned at him. "The hell she's your wife."

He dropped his mouth open as if he were surprised some more, but then he put his teeth together and his eyes narrowed. He started to speak, hesitated, then went ahead. I didn't like the look on his face. This was his last play, but I didn't know it yet, and he was so casual and convincing that if I

116

hadn't remembered him swearing at me and the hell he'd given me I might almost have believed him.

He started talking easily, but rapidly. "You're really mixed up, Mr. Scott. Come now, you don't need that gun." He laughed with what sounded like genuine amusement. "Of course Crystal is my wife. We were married here several months ago."

I didn't know at first why he was chatting like an old lady over the back fence, but right then he moved a little way toward his big black desk, and I got an inkling.

He went on, "And as for the sheriff—hell, Scott, I'll call him myself if it will make you happier." He laughed and moved casually toward his desk as if I didn't have a gun on him, and I knew, for sure, what all this apparently idle patter was for. He kept moving toward the desk, and I didn't stop him.

He continued, "We've got a big uproar between us for no reason. Believe me, there's no reason why we can't get along, Scott. We both got off on the wrong foot, that's all. And I honestly don't know what you're talking about. I don't even know any Carter or Freddy."

He kept talking away, hardly stopping for a breath, and that was the way for him to work it if he was going to be fool enough to try a hundred-to-one chance. Keep me listening, try to get me interested, not give me any opportunity even to interrupt his chatter while he kept it going and got closer, to the desk. Perhaps he might even make me start wondering for a moment if I *could* be wrong, get me off balance for the half second that might mean he had a way out.

Because his back was to the wall, and he must have known he was through and that there wasn't anything left to him except the last, desperate gamble. And Dante was first and foremost a gambler. This time he didn't have the edge he liked, but neither did he have a choice.

I took two steps closer to him as he reached the corner of the desk, because I knew he was going to try for a gun, and I said, "That's enough, Dante. Stop right there."

He acted as if he hadn't heard me. The almost pleasant expression stayed on his face and he continued, "If you want the sheriff here, fine. We can all sit around a table and clear this mess up." He shook his head. "And I can clear up any strange idea you've got about my marriage to Crystal right now. There's a copy of the license here."

He reached down to the top right drawer of his desk and pulled it open about a foot. I thumbed back the hammer of my gun as he moved, and the double click was loud in the sudden stillness of the office as he stopped speaking.

In that stillness I said, "Don't be a sucker, Dante. You haven't a chance."

117

But he did manage to catch me a little bit off balance. I'd expected him to slam the drawer open and dive for the gun, leaping to get out of the line of my fire, and swinging a gun up to blast at me. And he did nothing of the kind. He simply pulled the drawer open, then dropped his hand to his side and looked back at me. He said, "I don't understand, Mr. Scott. Chance for what?"

And because I hadn't expected that, I was a little bit off base at the next thing he did. It wasn't violent or a flurry of motion. He just straightened up and swung slightly to his right, and his left hand brushed the side of the open drawer as he looked over my left shoulder and grinned. It was a wide grin, almost a grimace, but it looked real enough. And looking past me to the door, he took one step toward me.

He didn't yell or push it too far, and maybe that's what did it. Or maybe it was because he actually stepped toward me while my cocked .38 was pointed straight at him. But he looked happy and confident, and there was a flashing fraction of a second in which I thought that this was the oldest gag in the world, and that it was old because it was good, and even while I knew damn well that nobody was there behind my back I still remembered that I hadn't bolted the door behind me when I'd hurried in here. I knew there was nobody behind me, but I also knew that if anybody *were* there I was dead sure as hell this time, and without looking around or turning I hunched my shoulders involuntarily and jumped a step to my right as the smile on Dante's face went away and he whirled and slammed his left hand into the drawer.

He was fast now that he'd started, and he had the gun in his hand and was dropping to his knees behind the desk as I got my feet planted solidly and pulled my gun back to bear on him.

Before I even squeezed down on the trigger he fired twice. Two shots that were almost one and that he couldn't have aimed, but just snapped at me in his haste, and while they slammed past me and the roar still filled the room I pulled the trigger of my gun once and started to squeeze it again, but that first shot sent a 158-grain lead slug crashing through the bone of his forehead and into his brain.

He fell back away from the desk and the gun slipped from his hand onto the carpet. He sprawled on his back and slowly, like a man relaxing instead of dying, his arms went limp and fell to the floor, and his legs, still bent at the knees, swayed apart in opposite directions, away from the center of his body. His heels slid downward a few inches along the carpet and stopped, and he lay there, awkwardly, with his eyes staring and blood just now bubbling from the hole in his forehead.

I looked down at him with my brain almost blank for those few seconds, and my teeth ground together till the muscles in my jaws ached, then I

118

snapped out of it and jumped to the door. I slammed the bolt home moments before footsteps pounded down the hall.

I ran across the room to the phone, scooped it up, and broke records getting through to the sheriff's office. Somebody yelled outside the door and I said into the phone, hardly caring who I was talking to, "I'm at the Inferno. Dante's office. Victor Dante's been shot and killed, and get the hell out here fast."

A comparatively calm voice at the other end of the line asked me who I was and what was happening, and I said into the phone, "This is Shell Scott. I'm at Dante's Inferno, in Dante's office. Dante is dead; I just shot him. Tell Hawkins and get out here fast before somebody else gets killed."

I didn't wait for an answer. I hung up the phone, went around behind the desk, and waited with my gun in my hand, as there was a muffled shout in the hallway and something heavy slammed into the door of the office.

20

THAT goddamned door was going to give. There was a regular hub-bub out there now. Shoulders slammed into the door and each time I could see it spring inward and the bolt quiver, getting ready to bust loose. Somebody crashed into the door again and it sprang half an inch inward, the wood splintering, and I knew the next one would do it.

In the comparative silence as whoever it was outside got ready to ram a shoulder into the door again, I yelled, "Hold it right there. I'll shoot hell out of the first man through."

Nobody slammed into the door. I realized then that the men outside couldn't know who or what was in here. All they could know was that there'd been shots, and then nobody had answered their shouts. They were out there thinking now, and I hoped to heaven they were slow thinkers. Because it wouldn't be long, unless whoever I'd called at the sheriff's office thought I was mad, till a couple of cars full of deputies came blasting out here.

Then it came, the biggest crash yet, and the door splintered as it gave all the way and swung around on its bent hinges to slam into the wall, and I dropped to one knee behind the desk, thinking, This is how Dante got it. I caught a confused blur of men outside in the hall and one man falling forward as he stumbled through the door and another man hunched over inside the room. I saw the gun in the hand of at least one man, but he didn't fire it and I didn't shoot, because then, as if the slamming of the door had set it off, we heard the shriek of the siren getting louder and closer, slurring down and then swinging up again in the horrid noise that was heavenly music. And then it was shrilling through the walls and dinning into our ears as another siren whined a counterpoint behind it and, at least for now, the shooting was over.

I was going to compliment the Clark County sheriff's department on its efficiency even if the deputies beat a tattoo on my skull, each and every one of them. And they might.

Sheriff's deputies came pouring in and people milled around in the hall and gasped in the casino, and it was as if I had another parade. Only this one wasn't going anywhere; it was standing in one spot and jumping up and down with a red face, jumping up and down on one spot, and that was the spot I was on. This was a big one, for sure.

But the deputies got things under control quickly and efficiently. They knew their jobs and they did them in a hurry. And pretty soon I was looking at Hawkins, and Hawkins was looking at me, and it occurred to me in a flash that I was not the fair-haired boy.

Time passed excruciatingly. We were still in Dante's office. And so were three other arms of the law. I'd been talking to Lieutenant Hawkins for forty-five minutes, but only about what had happened in this room. Now I said, "Believe me, Hawkins, I told Dante before this thing exploded that I was phoning the sheriff's department and turning him over to you."

He sucked on his teeth. "And for what was it again?"

"For murder."

"Seems like the smart thing would have been to call us before you came here."

"Maybe it would have. But you'll understand why I didn't when I—explain the rest of it."

"The rest?" The deep creases alongside his nose got deeper as he frowned.

I looked at my watch: twelve-fifty A.M. This conversation was taking time, too much time. I knew that there was a plane due to land here in twenty minutes or less, and that J. Harrison Bing would be on it, headed for Dante's desert home. This damned thing could still blow up in my face, and I might learn all about the state prison at Carson City. From the inside.

"Hawkins," I said, "we've spent a lot of time jawing about this, but it's only covered the last hour or so. There's more, but I'd have to go back over three days to get it all in." I stopped and thought about what I'd say next, thought

121

about it for fifteen dragging seconds while Hawkins stared at me, then I said, "This is one hell of a story you're going to hear. One hell of a story. And this may sound silly, but I don't have time to tell every bit of it this minute." He opened his mouth, but I hurried on. "I'll *tell* it; I'll tell it all, and I'll tell it any way you want. But my way you'll like it a lot better." I went on after what I hoped was a significant pause. "About this here in the office. I told you down at the court house that Dante was trying to kill me. Well, he tried it himself and I shot him."

He yawned, but that didn't fool me into thinking he was sleepy. He said, "A man could tell me that so he could shoot a guy and then claim self-defense."

"A man could if he was nuts," I said. "I shot Dante after he tossed two slugs at me, and if I *hadn't* shot him you'd be out here looking at holes in my face." I paused a moment and then said, "I take that back. I meant holes in my face and my back, and you'd be looking at me in the desert if you found me at all. Like William Carter. Because ever since right after I hit this town Dante's been trying to kill me."

Hawkins said, "Two shots he took at you? First? Any witnesses?"

"Yeah. No people, but two bullets in the wall that was behind me when he shot at me, nitrate particles in Dante's left hand that will show up in a paraffin test and prove he *did* fire a gun, and a hole in his brain. He didn't do any shooting at me after he grew that hole; he did it before."

Hawkins stuck his tongue in his cheek, let it rove around a little, and sighed.

I said, "There's one more act in this business. If you'll let me go—take me—to Dante's home in the desert, I can explain a whole lot of things that have happened in the last three days and more: Carter in the desert; Freddy Powell at the airport in my Cadillac; a couple of bruised muscle men at McCarran Field, a couple of Dante's men at the Desert Inn—one, named Lloyd, with a knife in him, and the other one dead. And there's more. But we've got to get out to Dante's home before the next plane lands at the airport. Dante's not going to do any explaining."

Hawkins' eyes just kept getting wider and wider and wider. It was eight to five he thought one of Dante's bullets had gone in my ear and was rattling around inside there. But I told him we had to get going fast, and that it was all his case, he could have it, and I'd give him enough so maybe he could hang me. I screamed at the top of my lungs that otherwise I'd clam up instanter or just fall down on the floor and die and he could guess what I'd been talking about, and that we had to hurry, there wasn't time for an advance blow-by-blow account now. So we went. Three uniformed deputies and Hawkins. And the prisoner: me.

It was fifteen minutes after one in the morning by the time we got to the desert house and walked up to the front door. The house was dark, and my heart was flapping against my lips while Hawkins rang the bell. If the place was empty I could kiss Los Angeles good-by, because I'd be in Nevada a long, long time. I hadn't been kidding Hawkins when I told him there wasn't time for a blow-by-blow account, but I'd had another reason for not spilling all I knew back there at the Inferno.

Then lights went on inside and I saw little Blondie coming to the door with more on than when I'd last seen her, and I almost flipped with relief. Because even if I wasn't out of the woods yet, I could see the prairies ahead. And *now* I could fire my ammunition at Hawkins. If J. Harrison Bing had arrived ahead of us and Blondie had taken a powder, then I could have chattered at Hawkins till my tongue came loose and flew away like a bird, and it might not have done any good; he'd have been devilish hard to convince. Now, though, I had a chance. And Bing was due any minute, because by now his plane was in.

She opened the door and we walked inside. I waited till we were all in and she was still sputtering, half asleep and shocked and surprised, then I said to Hawkins, "Now I can talk for hours. And I will."

Then I turned to her and I said, "Hello, Isabel. I've been looking all over hell for you." And while she stared at me coldly I said to Hawkins, "Here's the tomato who put three little holes in William Carter's back."

Isabel gasped and Hawkins stepped toward her. Looking through the window behind his back, I could see headlights tearing up the road from Highway 91, almost to the house now.

I turned back to Isabel. "I phoned your father earlier," I said. "There's been a lot of hell because of you and he's got a right to be here. Besides, I wanted it this way."

There was a trace of panic in her blue eyes, but she was pretty much under control. She said, "I didn't kill anyone. I don't understand. My name isn't even Isabel."

She looked cute as hell, still, but I didn't like her very well. Those were the first words she'd ever spoken to me, and she'd told me three lies. And she understood, all right. I understood something, too: The way this was shaping up, she was one of the most cold-blooded bitches I'd ever run across.

Then the car pulled to a stop outside and her father came running up on the porch and inside, and I took a very good look at him as he came in.

Because I'd never seen this fat old pappy before.

21

J. HARRISON BING pulled two hundred and twenty pounds to a stop inside the door, and panting, said, "Who called me? Which of you? What—" He stopped and frowned, looking around him. "What is this? Why all these men?" He looked at Blondie and said, "Isabel, what's going on?"

It was getting to her, piling up on her, and that was partly what I was counting on: Bust out of the night with no warning and throw it at her fast, one thing after another, a little like Dante had tried to throw conversation at me a while back. Only I'd stacked everything I could in my favor. This was a rough way to do it, but it's worse lying in a desert, with blood on your mouth, or having part of a Cadillac blown through your chest.

I said, "Mr. Bing, this is Lieutenant Hawkins. He's out here to arrest your daughter for murder."

I didn't like what that did to his face, but I liked what happened to hers. Because maybe I was brutal, but I had my back against the wall, too. This one was for keeps, and some of it had to spill out of Isabel's pretty mouth.

She spoke rapidly, in a voice that was a little shrill. "You're insane! I haven't killed anyone. I'm Mrs. Victor Dante. None of this makes sense, not any of it."

"Your father's right here to help make a liar out of you," I said.

Mr. Bing broke in. "See here, what's this all about? There must be some mistake." He was still shocked and his fleshy red face was pained. He looked at me. "Are you the one who called me? I don't know you."

"We've never met. Your son-in-law hired me, pretending to be you, and gave me one of your business cards. That's how I reached you tonight. I'm sorry about this, sir, but there isn't any mistake." I paused momentarily, then asked him, "You *can* prove you're J. Harrison Bing, can't you?"

"Of course I can prove it. What—"

"This is your daughter, isn't it? It's important."

He sighed, looked at the uniformed deputies, and answered, "Yes, she's my daughter."

"She and Harvey Ellis were never divorced, were they?"

"Why, no. I don't understand. Why ask me that?"

I glanced at Hawkins and back to Bing, and hesitated. After a moment Hawkins spoke softly to one of the deputies, who came over to Bing and took him outside.

I turned to Isabel. "You'll feel better if you start talking about it now, Mrs. Ellis."

"I'm not Mrs. Ellis. And there's nothing to talk about."

"Look," I said quietly, "of course you're Mrs. Ellis. Your father just said you were, and you know we can prove it other ways now. Fingerprints, old friends." I paused and added, "We can even bring Harvey up here."

Her face went a little blank at that. She started to say something, stopped for several seconds, then said, "I. . . divorced Harvey. And I haven't killed anybody."

"The hell you divorced him. You *couldn't*, Isabel. And that helps explain why you killed Carter." She opened her mouth again but I kept talking. "You were sure as hell married to Ellis when he went to San Quentin over a year ago. That felony conviction gave you grounds for divorce, all right, but it takes over a year to get a final decree in California, baby—and you married Dante long before that year was up."

There was more than a trace of panic in her eyes now, and she slowly closed her mouth and didn't say anything. She looked rattled enough so that I might get away with a bluff. I stepped up close to her and said roughly, "Maybe you don't understand how much we know. Listen to this, Isabel: When your husband got out of prison he started looking for you—you know why—and he was anxious enough to hire detectives when he couldn't find you himself. He used your father's name so there wouldn't be any trail from you back to one Harvey Ellis, but also so that you might not guess your husband was breathing down your neck. He had to have a reason for that, didn't he, Isabel?"

She was biting on her lower lip, and her breasts rose and fell with her rapid breathing. I kept it going. "When it figured that my client wasn't really your father, you can guess what I did, can't you, Isabel? I phoned Ellis and had quite a chat with him."

She gasped, then her eyes widened as she pressed her lips together. That was enough for me. I said, "The L.A. police had already told me they suspected you'd turned your own husband in. And Harvey Ellis could certainly figure out who sent him to prison—especially when she stopped writing him and disappeared. He told me who turned him in, Isabel."

I grinned down at her and she said frantically, "That doesn't mean anything. What if I did? It doesn't mean I'd kill anyone. Why would I—"

I broke in on her. "I'll tell you why, honey. Bigamy, for one, and prison for you—among other and maybe better reasons. Hell, Isabel, it's obvious now. When Carter showed up here and got a look at you, it was all over. Incidentally, baby, the gun you shot him with must be around somewhere. That can be traced."

She was shaking her head back and forth, but I didn't stop. I said rapidly, "We can even ignore the bigamy angle. You must have known, or learned, that Carter had been hired by your husband, and you certainly couldn't afford to let him go back and tell Ellis where you were. Ellis wasn't going to kiss you after you'd sent him to prison, left him flat, sold his home, maybe stolen him blind, and God knows what else. Honey, *that's* why you couldn't go ahead and get a divorce up here after you got your six weeks in: because hubby was already out of the can when you'd established residence, and the divorce summons would have told him where you were. If he were still in prison, where he couldn't get at you, it wouldn't have made any difference; but with hubby out, you couldn't go ahead. He'd have found you without hiring detectives."

I stopped and looked at her as her eyes darted around the room, from Hawkins to the uniformed deputies and back to me. I said, "What were you going to do? Get rid of Ellis, then marry Dante again, legally? It all fits now, Isabel. When Dante fell for you at the Pelican and popped the question, you'd already changed your name and appearance so you could drop out of sight and lose Ellis for good. Becoming Mrs. Dante would really complete the switch. Anyway, you married him—as Crystal Claire. There's another reason for killing Carter. If Dante ever learned what you'd done to one husband, and that you were still legally married to Ellis, he'd have known you weren't the

126

sweet little twenty-six-year-old bachelor gal you claimed to be. Dante just isn't the kind of guy who'd enjoy being taken for a ride. You want more? You want to tell us about Carter now?"

"No. . . there's nothing." It didn't sound like her voice at all any more. She knew by now that even if I didn't have every bit of it, I had enough.

I said, "Hasn't it been on your mind? Who dumped Carter in the desert? Dante? He was covering up for you at the Pelican when I walked in on him there, so you must have told him about it. What kind of lies did you tell him to explain your killing Carter? And what's Dante going to think when he knows your real reasons for murder? And how did it feel to shoot a man three times in the back? A man with a nice little wife and a kid in Los Angeles."

She put her hands over her ears and started to turn away, but she wasn't talking yet. She still hadn't admitted a thing, and I still wasn't out of the woods, so I stepped even closer to her, grabbed her wrists, and pulled her hands down. Her face was inches from mine and her white skin was even paler than it had been a minute before. Her lips were parted and dry, and I could tell she was ready to go now, on her way. So I broke it off in her, and I didn't like it a hell of a lot but I made myself look into her upturned blue eyes as I gave her the last of it.

"There's no help for you, baby; not even from Dante. It's no good now, no happy-ever-after, but Dante never did know you were playing him for a sucker."

She frowned a little, her eyes puzzled, and I continued softly, "He never even knew you weren't Crystal Claire. He still thought you were his sweet little Crystal when I killed him."

Her face sagged and she blinked into my eyes, then she let her gaze slip down to my chest and slowly back up to my face again, and I said, "It's true, baby; all over. Just a little while ago I shot and killed Victor Dante."

And that was the one that did it. She swung her blonde head over toward Hawkins and saw the answer in his face, and I hammered the one question about Carter at her, and the answer spilled, twisted, out of her mouth. Not much, just the age-old "Oh, my God, I did. I killed him," and then for the second time since I'd first seen her she fainted dead away.

I was a brutal son of a bitch, but those prairies were closer now, and maybe I was climbing over the bodies to get there, but I was getting there.

Fifteen minutes later, as I watched Isabel's face and listened to her talk, I realized she was even more selfish and cold-blooded than I'd thought. She'd been money-hungry even when, at seventeen, she'd married a man twenty years older than herself, and finally, as has happened before and will happen again, Harvey Ellis had stolen to buy his little Isabel the things she'd craved. He'd done a hell of a good job of it, too. Captain Samson had mentioned wondering if Ellis might have got his hands on that quarter of a million dollars that had been lifted in L.A. Sam had wondered right, and there'd been almost $260,000 in the Harvey-Isabel kitty when Isabel finally got good and bitchy.

She continued almost as if she were talking to herself. "I wanted that money more than I'd ever wanted anything and I wanted to get rid of the old goat. I practically begged him to pull one more job, then I turned him in and filed for a California divorce. I changed my name and all, but I was afraid to start spending the money because of the cops. I still had it when I met Dante, and he was—well, he was all the answers, and I could use all that money easy, through him. He was crazy about me, too. Anyway, I married him and let him use the money to help finance his Inferno deal." She paused and smiled slightly. "He thought I gave it to him because I was nuts about him." The smile went away and she continued, "After—after Carter, I told Victor that I'd done it for him, because I loved him. I told him Carter had found out that Victor killed Big Jim White, and that he was going to the sheriff when I. . . stopped him."

Hawkins interrupted her there. "Dante killed Big Jim."

She didn't even look up. "It can't hurt him now," she said. "He killed him. Just before he stepped into the Inferno deal. Carter didn't know any more about it than anyone else, but Victor believed me." She stopped for a moment and then added, "He really did love me."

She went on talking, then went over it again, only the second time through she tried to make us believe that Carter had attempted to blackmail her. It would have been a sweet setup for blackmail, but it seemed to me like too much of an afterthought on Isabel's part. At least I had a better idea now why Dante must have come close to jumping clear up to the moon when I'd walked in on him and Lorraine at the Pelican. With Carter dead, if somebody—me, for instance—should start looking for him, that somebody might not only prove Isabel murdered Carter, but also stumble onto the same information Dante thought Carter had possessed. Isabel kept talking and we got it all, but it was a long night. Especially for Isabel.

The sun was up and Isabel was in a cell when I finished talking to a tired and red-eyed Hawkins.

"How about me?" I asked him.

"Like I told you before," he said wearily, "the only crimes that aren't bailable in Nevada are treason and first-degree murder. You get bail, but it'll be high."

I was so worn out and sleepy it was hard to think straight, but I knew there was something I'd been meaning to do. Then I remembered. "Use your phone?" I asked Hawkins.

He shoved the phone across the desk and I called the Desert Inn and got put through to Colleen's room. Her voice was sleepy when she answered.

"Hello, there," I said. "I didn't think about your being asleep." Just saying the word made my eyes droop.

"Shell? Is that you?"

"Uh-huh. Look, it's all finished. I'll be going down to L.A. tonight, but I'll have to come back up in a couple of days for a coroner's inquest."

"What happened? Are you all right?"

"Yeah. I've been going over the thing all night; I don't think I could run through it again right now, Colleen."

There was a little pause while I blinked sleepily at the far wall, then she said, "You're going back to L.A.? You're going to stop and see me, though, aren't you?"

"Oh, sure," I said. I was thinking that after the binge I'd been on, topped by this past night, I might have to be carried to Colleen's room, but I'd sure as hell get there. I added, "If I can make it, that is." I yawned. "Look, honey, why don't we go down together? You want to—"

I stopped. Right in the middle of my yawn there'd been a click in my ear. It suddenly occurred to me that Colleen had, for no reason at all, hung up on me. I looked at Hawkins with my mouth open.

He was grinning. "You sure kill the ladies," he said.

"What happened? She hung up. What—"

Hawkins said in a sticky voice, "I'll see you, dahling. That is, if I can make it, dahling." He sounded like Tallulah, but I got it, and I groaned.

"Hell," I said, "I meant I was so beat—" I turned it off. There was no point in explaining to Hawkins. I phoned again, but there wasn't any answer. What the hell? Now I'd have to clear all misunderstandings away like magic when I got back to the hotel.

I couldn't leave yet, though, so we sat quietly for a while smoking cigarettes that didn't taste good because we'd already had too many. And I had a not very pleasant taste in my mouth, anyway. Hawkins had brought me up to date on what I didn't know. Nils Abel, whose bald skull I'd cracked at the airport, actually *did* have a cracked skull and was in the hospital; his chum, Joe Fine, was going to be picked up; and bushy-haired Lloyd, whose last name I finally learned was Weaver, hadn't died from that knife in his middle, but he was a very sick man—and was now talking a blue streak.

As for me, Hawkins was convinced that none of my "flights" had been to avoid prosecution but had merely been considered attempts to live another day. And he didn't mind having the Big Jim file closed, either. I had plenty to answer for, but Hawkins assured me that a "justifiable homicide" verdict by the coroner's jury was almost a foregone conclusion and there probably wouldn't even be a preliminary hearing.

129

I thought about that, and about the people in the case. Funny thing. Isabel would have a hard time blaming anybody but herself for the mess she was in—and Harvey Ellis hadn't even violated his parole. I knew now that all the things Ellis had said he'd told Carter were actually things Carter had learned and told him, but it had fooled me for a while. I thought some more about Isabel and what she was up against, and even though I knew she deserved anything she got from a jury, and even though there was little chance that she'd be sentenced to death, I couldn't help feeling glad they used gas for executions in Nevada.

No matter what she'd done, I sure would have hated the thought of Isabel getting the chair.

22

HOLLYWOOD looked good to me, as it always does after I've been away for a while, but I felt, in a word, lousy. I'd sold my sweet old Cad for junk before I caught the late-afternoon flight from Las Vegas and left the fourth and final day of Helldorado behind, and that was a good reason for feeling low, but there was a better one. Even the fact that I had $1,900 in my pants—fee, bonus, and some unusual expenses—didn't cheer me up much. After reaching L.A. I'd stopped off to see Ellis at the address Sam had listed in his telegram, and collected my entire fee before I'd spilled a word to Ellis about his "daughter." Then I'd left and the plain-clothes men had taken over to ask new questions about $260,000. None of that had cheered me up, though, because when I'd finally got back to the Desert Inn before I left Las Vegas, Colleen was gone. Her room had already been rented to somebody else, and the clerk at the desk told me she'd checked out.

I couldn't understand it. Even if Colleen had misinterpreted my sleepy words on the phone, I couldn't imagine her flying off in a huff. I'd thought she was made of more solid and sensible stuff than that. And, I had to admit it, I really did miss her.

131

I got out of the taxi that had brought me to the Spartan Apartment Hotel and went inside. I stopped at the desk and asked Corky for my key. He grinned at me. "Oh, sure, you're some card." Then he peered at me and his face grew a surprised look. "Didn't you—Oh, no."

I blinked at him. "What's the matter? All I asked for was my key."

"It's up there. I thought—"

I didn't wait for him to finish. I spun around and sprinted up the steps to the second floor three at a time. I ran down to my rooms and slammed the door open and stepped inside. She was there, all right. Damn her to hell, she was there, and I was surprised at how good I felt when I saw her. There was a dryness in my throat and my heart pounded with the excitement of seeing her again.

Colleen was sitting on the oversized chocolate divan that's almost straight in front of the door of my apartment, and she looked up and smiled when I came in. She held a half-empty highball glass in her right hand and she leaned back on the divan and waved the glass at me. "Hi," she said. "Thought you'd never get here."

"Damn you," I said. "Damn you to pieces. What's the idea of worrying hell out of me? I thought you were mad at me. I thought I'd never see you again."

She was smiling. "That's the *idea*," she said gleefully.

I grinned at her, walked over, and sat down on the divan beside her. "So you're a smart one, huh? Scheming at me. Then you weren't really angry?"

"But I was. I was furious. I packed and almost checked out before I woke up—literally—and realized how silly I was being. But I checked out anyway and drove down here. You'd told me where you lived and also promised to show me Los Angeles." She stopped and smiled at me. "I figured if you were going to worry about me at all, it was time you started. Can't have you getting lost in rooms all night like you did."

I knew what she meant. Blast her, would she *never* forget that Lorraine business? I pointed at the glass in her hand and changed the subject. "Uh-huh," I said. "Stealing."

"You said any time people come to see you, you want them to make themselves at home. I do what I'm told, Mr. Scott."

"That's encouraging." I hoped it was, because she looked wonderful. She'd apparently spent some time prettying herself up after the drive from Vegas, and she'd done a terrific job. She was barefooted, with her bare legs curled underneath her, but she was wearing a vivid green velvet gown that emphasized everything she had, and she had everything. A man could look from that face with its wide-eyed innocence to that ye-gods body and get dizzy. I got a little dizzy. I could tell she still wasn't wearing a brassiere, and I couldn't help wondering about those black frilly things I'd seen her pick up in her room at the Desert Inn, and wondering if something like that were under the green velvet.

"Get that look off your face," she said.

I cleared my throat. "Where's my drink?"

She jumped up and padded on bare feet across the thick shag nap of my yellow-gold carpet and disappeared in the kitchenette. She was back after some glook, glook, glook sounds out there and handed me a tall drink.

"I'm ahead," she said. "Whee!"

I grinned at her. "I'll catch up."

Colleen sat down on the divan again and, leaning forward, poked me in the chest with a red fingernail. "Since you're taking me out," she said, "how do I look? Is this gown too daring for Los Angeles?"

"Not too daring for me. But the vice squad will have you in the back room grilling you."

She giggled. By George, she was ahead. I pulled lustily on my highball, then said, "I'll drink this and get ready."

"No more work? All done?"

"All done for now. Case solved. You helped, Colleen."

"Me? How?"

"Talking about divorces and six weeks' residence and what a funny name Isabel Bing was and so on. That was up in your room when I wanted you to come out and let me dry your back."

She smiled. "I remember."

"You were in the shower and I wondered if you could possibly have a scar on your—on you, and I put that with your talk, and with a card on the dresser that was the only proof I had that a man was who he said he was, and no wonder he didn't get any letters, and then I knew you didn't have a scar."

"You're ahead of *me*," she said.

I grinned. "Then when I learned that little Isabel had a scar and had bleached her hair, it was settled."

"Who?"

"Mrs. Dante."

"How do you know she bleached her hair?"

"My goodness," I said. "My drink's empty." I got up and went to the kitchenette and made another.

"Answer me," Colleen said.

"It'll take me a few minutes to shower and get ready."

"We're off!" she said. She looked at her wrist watch. "You'd better hurry. It's after nine already. I saved time by getting dressed. Oh, I used your shower. You mind?"

"You can use anything that's mine. Seems like we go through life taking showers almost together. Have another drink. Make two. I'll be finished with this one in a minute."

She scurried into the kitchenette and I piled into the bathroom, finished my drink, undressed, and climbed into the shower. In a minute Colleen was banging on the door.

"Come on in," I yelled happily.

"You decent?"

"You kidding? Come on in."

I had the shower curtain pulled across the entrance to the shower, and in a moment a white hand holding a very brown drink snaked around the curtain's edge. I grabbed the drink, then stuck my head outside and looped the heavy cloth under my chin.

"Colleen, tell me something," I said. "When I first saw you at the bar in the Desert Inn I looked at your face and thought it was one of the most beautiful, most innocent-looking faces I'd ever seen. Then I wandered afield and my spine crinkled. Tell me, which is the real you?"

She laughed, backed up one step, then pursed her lips and blew me a kiss. Then she laughed again and went into the living room. I didn't know exactly what that meant, but I was sure as hell getting out of this shower.

I turned around and warm water squirted into my highball, and it struck me that this particular happening had never happened before. I jerked my glass out of the stream of water and eyed it for a moment. I was drinking these dark brown drinks awfully fast, but there seemed nothing to do but finish it, so I finished it. I sat the empty glass in the soap rack and broke into a chorus of "I Wish I Could Shimmy Like My Sister Kate" as I finished soaping, rinsed off, climbed out, and toweled down.

With the big Turkish bath towel wrapped securely around me I strode toward the bedroom and clean clothes, but stopped a few feet before I got there. I looked over at Colleen.

"'Lo," I said.

"You get dressed!"

Ahh, she was a sly one. I said, "Sure. But how about one more drink first?"

"Well," she said hesitantly, "all right."

I walked over and sat down—carefully on the divan. Colleen brought me another highball and sat down beside me.

"Whee!" she said.

"Whee. Whee you want—I mean, where you want to go first?"

"What'd you suggest?"

"Strip."

She shook her head. "Impossible," she said. "Impossible, impossible."

134

"Sunset Strip. Mocambo, Ciro's, Shmiro's," I said. "Finish our drinks, I'll get ready, and we'll go. O.K.?"

"You'd better get ready. You can't go like that!"

I leered at her. Right in front of the divan is a big, low, black-lacquered coffee table with water rings on its top. I placed my still full glass on the table, carefully maneuvering it so that I would get it exactly on one of the old rings. Colleen watched this, fascinated.

I blinked at her. "Clever?"

"Clever. Kiss me."

"What?" Must have been those three fast bourbons, but I said it again. "What?"

"All this time," she said lightly, "and you haven't kissed me."

She was about two feet away from me on the divan. At first. She leaned closer, her arms sliding sinuously around my neck, and her lips moved slightly, her eyes narrowed just a trifle, and she raised an eyebrow no more than a fraction of an inch, but the same things happened again to my spine.

Both her clenched fists met at the back of my neck and she pulled me toward her, and she must have been surprised at how easily I pulled, and then her lips were pressed against mine. I raised my hands to her shoulders and started to slide them around to her back, but she pulled her head away and laughed softly in my face.

"This is me," she said.

I looked at her for long seconds, my eyes inches from hers as the smile slowly faded from her face, and suddenly, right then, all the light banter ended. Always up until now we'd been joking with each other, never really serious, but that was over in this moment and we both knew it, knew it for sure. I could see it in the almost sullen, narrow-eyed look that came over her face, and hear it in the quick intake of her breath, and feel it in the pressure of her fingernails as they pressed into the skin of my back. We weren't playing our usual game with words and innuendoes any more; honesty and wanting were between us for quiet, brittle moments as we looked at each other, neither of us smiling now.

When I slid my arms around her she came eagerly to me, her eyes closed, the long dark lashes trembling, and her mouth raised toward me as I bent my head to hers, and then her lips were warm and alive on mine, caressing, squeezing, moist, clinging. It was, again, as it had been before when I kissed her, but this was an even more complete giving of herself, a more frenzied intimacy that sent a weakness through all my body at the warm touch of her. With a kind of hunger I kissed her again and again on her blood-full, curving lips and the corners of her closed eyes while she whispered almost unintelligible words against my mouth and cheek, and the desire that had been smoldering in me ever since I had first seen her swelled and pulsed like fire, hotly inside me.

135

Colleen was softer, warmer, more desiring, and more desired than I had imagined even she would be. She pulled her mouth from mine and let her head hang back as she whispered my name, the white smoothness of her throat before me, and I pressed my lips to the hollow where the blood pulsed close to the surface, felt the beat of her heart against my lips as I kissed her throat and the white mound of her breast. Her hands pulled me close to her, pressed my mouth tight against her breast as she whispered, "Shell, oh, darling, darling. . . love me. . ."

I picked her up in my arms and carried her into the near darkness of the bedroom and lowered her gently to the bed. Her eyes were wide, staring up at me, and her breath came rapidly between her parted lips as I sank down beside her and curled my fingers in the velvet cloth at her shoulders.

"Wait," she whispered. She reached quickly with her hands and in a moment wriggled free of the green gown, and then a wisp of frilly blackness slid noiselessly over the pale gleam of her thighs and dropped to the floor. Completely naked now, she lay quietly with her arms at her sides, the palms of her hands up and the fingers curling. As I leaned toward her, the rounded whiteness of her arms went convulsively around me, her nails tracing shivering paths over the skin of my back, and she whispered tightly, "Love me, Shell," then over and over again, "Love me, love me, love me," until my mouth muffled the words and finally stilled them.

She lay motionless for a moment with her eyes closed and her breathing rapid and heavy while my lips caressed her throat and descended slowly to the brazen fullness of her bare breasts, my fingertips gentle against the smooth firmness of her thigh and the swelling curve of her hip, and then her fingers dug into my shoulders when my mouth found hers again, and she pressed her teeth into my lips as I caressed the soft, warm, myriad-curved length of her, and then there was only the intimate caress of her tongue against mine, and her fingers clutching at my flesh, and her yielding body writhing against me.

I turned on the small table lamp at the side of the bed and lit two cigarettes for us, and we talked for a few minutes in half sentences and soft phrases, our voices, like our bodies, relaxed and lazy. Little by little the languor left us and the conversation was laced with smiles and soft laughter. Finally Colleen sat up on the bed and stretched luxuriously, arching her back and thrusting her arms high over her head.

I grinned at her. "Hussy. You're absolutely shameless. Besides being wonderful. Also, this is the first time I've seen you with your hair down. I like it."

She looked at me and smiled, then put both hands behind her head and shoved a mass of long, red hair forward over her face. "Shameless hair," she said. "Kind of a tangle, isn't it?"

136

"Looks good," I said. "*You* look good. You look wild. You look wicked. You can still fix your hair—and we can still go out. I promised to show you the town, Colleen, and I hereby promise to keep my promise." I grinned at her. "At least we can catch the last show."

She tossed her head and blew at a few stray strands of hair, then looked at me again. "Why, you silly," she said. "Who wants to go out?"

ABOUT THE AUTHOR

RICHARD S. PRATHER was the author of the world-famous Shell Scott detective series, which has over forty million copies in print in the United States and many millions more in hundreds of foreign-anguage editions. There are forty-one volumes, including four collections of short stories and novelettes. In 1986, Prather was awarded the Private Eye Writers of America's Life Achievement Award for his contributions to the detective genre. He and his wife, Tina, lived among the beautiful Red Rocks of Sedona, Arizona. He enjoyed organic gardening, gin on the rocks, and golf. He collected books on several different life-enriching subjects and occasionally reread his own books with huge enjoyment, especially *Strip for Murder*. Prather died on February 14, 2007.

OPEN ROAD
INTEGRATED MEDIA

Open Road Integrated Media is a digital publisher and multimedia content company. Open Road creates connections between authors and their audiences by marketing its ebooks through a new proprietary online platform, which uses premium video content and social media.

CPSIA information can be obtained
at www.ICGtesting.com
Printed in the USA
LVHW041914200319
611291LV00001B/31/P